The showe[r

Much smaller [illegible]

shared at the Stallion family home.

Stepping into the flow of heated water Travis pressed his hands to Tierra's shoulders, moving his body close to hers. His fingers skated down the length of her arms, tickling her flesh.

Tierra closed her eyes as she moved against him, pressing her back up against his chest. A shiver raced from the pit of her stomach and into her limbs. She felt a delightful throb between her legs.

Tilting her face to his, Tierra kissed him. Their lips touched first, then their tongues, meeting like old friends. Their passion rose in intensity, his tongue eagerly searching her mouth, reaching as far as it could. Tierra moaned as Travis danced in her mouth then gently sucked on her lips. He couldn't remember ever having tasted anything so sweet.

Tierra opened her eyes wide, staring deep into his. In that moment she couldn't imagine wanting to be anywhere more than where she was right now. More important, she knew she didn't have to.

"I want you," Tierra murmured before kissing his mouth again.

Books by Deborah Fletcher Mello

Kimani Romance

In the Light of Love
Always Means Forever
To Love a Stallion
Tame a Wild Stallion
Lost in a Stallion's Arms
Promises to a Stallion

Kimani Arabesque

Forever and a Day
The Right Side of Love
A Love for All Time
Take Me to Heart

DEBORAH FLETCHER MELLO

has been writing since she was thirteen and can't imagine doing anything else. Her first romance novel, *Take Me to Heart,* earned her a 2004 Romance Slam Jam nomination for Best New Author. In 2005 she received Slam Jam's Book of the Year and Favorite Heroine nominations for her novel *The Right Side of Love,* and in 2009 she won a *RT Book Reviews* Reviewers' Choice Award for her ninth novel, *Tame a Wild Stallion.*

For Deborah, writing is akin to breathing, and she firmly believes that if she could not write she would cease to exist. Weaving a story that leaves her audience feeling full and complete, as if they've just enjoyed an incredible meal, is the ultimate thrill for her. Born and raised in Connecticut, Deborah now maintains base camp in North Carolina but considers home to be wherever the moment finds her.

Deborah Fletcher Mello

To the late Mrs. Hattie Joanne Woody, who demanded excellence, nurtured greatness, instilled compassion, and inspired a generation of dreamers to reach beyond the stars.

Your love thrives in your son's heart and I am grateful for it.

KIMANI PRESS™

Recycling programs for this product may not exist in your area.

ISBN-13: 978-0-373-86175-0

PROMISES TO A STALLION

www.kimanipress.com

Printed in U.S.A.

Dear Reader,

It's raining men, Stallion-style! Those billionaire brothers Matthew, Mark, Luke and John Stallion are back and this time they're riding with family cousin Travis Stallion, another stud who definitely doesn't disappoint.

I absolutely loved writing Travis and Tierra's story. Inspired by a real-life love story, I couldn't help but imagine the possibilities of a couple meeting, falling in love and making the decision to marry in less than thirty days.

Thank you for taking this amazing journey with me. Your words of encouragement and support continue to keep me writing and motivate me to write well.

I always love to hear what you think so please feel free to contact me at DeborahMello@aol.com.

Until the next time, take care and God bless.

With much love,

Deborah Fletcher Mello
www.deborahmello.blogspot.com

Chapter 1

Every head in the room turned to stare at the beautiful young woman who had just released an unnerving scream at the top of her lungs. Startled expressions turned into curious stares, and a few amused smiles, that swept from corner to corner as the other patrons of Ridgeland Diner noted her infectious smile. Something had obviously made the woman extremely happy.

Seated at a cushioned booth, Tierra Braddy was jumping excitedly in her seat. Clearly embarrassed, the man seated beside her looked around sheepishly. He was hardly impressed, but his twenty-eight-year-old baby sister was fully taken by the good news she had heard.

"Girlfriend, you are the best," Tierra exclaimed into her BlackBerry. Her deep brown gaze met the dark eyes that resembled her own. She was grinning widely, but her brother's full lips were turned into a deep frown. She poked her tongue out at him as she continued her cell phone conversation. “Thank you. Thank you so much,” she said just before disconnecting the call she’d been so eagerly engaged in.

“Let me guess,” Tingin Braddy said, leaning back against his seat, his arms folding over his broad chest. “You were able to pull off a dozen gold-winged doves for this wedding of the century?”

Tierra’s eyes widened in delight. “Better. We are confirmed for the chapel at Briscoe Ranch. Isn’t that great?” she exclaimed, her whole body quivering with excitement. “You remember Eden Waller, don’t you? She married Doug Waller’s brother Jack.”

“I remember Doug. I don’t think I ever met Jack or his wife.”

Tierra shrugged. “Well, Eden and her sister are the event planners at Briscoe Ranch, and they weren’t sure the renovations would be completed in time for us to use it. But she said they are officially finished and mine will be the first wedding in the building since 1949! How great is that!”

“Grand,” Tingin responded, no hint of enthusiasm in his voice. “But let me ask you something very important,” he said, leaning forward in his seat and resting his elbows atop the table. He leaned his chin against the back of his cupped hands and met her curious stare evenly. “Are you sure about this, Tea? Because it’s not too late to change your mind.”

“I can’t believe you would ask me something like that!” The young woman’s voice was laced with attitude. “I have been planning my dream wedding since I was ten years old. That’s how sure I am.”

“I get the dream wedding part, kiddo. We were all

just hoping you'd find a dream groom to go with those nuptials."

"Don't start, Tingin," Tierra said, the hint of a reprimand on her tongue. "Don't spoil this for me. You know how I feel about Damien."

"That's not the problem, either. It's how Damien feels about you that has me concerned."

The smile on Tierra's face had folded down into an annoyed frown. "Big brother, be in a relationship that lasts longer than a minute and then you can have a conversation with me about somebody loving somebody." Her negative attitude had magnified substantially.

Tingin held up his hands as if in defeat. "My apologies. Don't get your spine all bent out of shape. I wouldn't be a good big brother if I didn't ask, Tierra."

"You always have to try and spoil things, Tingin. Ever since we were little kids. You get some perverse thrill out of trying to burst my bubbles, don't you?"

The man laughed heartily. "You have me all figured out. I've been plotting since the day you were born to bring you down," he said sarcastically.

Tierra punched her brother in the arm, the gesture just hard enough to get his full and undivided attention. "Well, stop. It's not working."

"Ouch, that hurt." Tingin rubbed his upper arm.

"It was supposed to. Now," Tierra said, changing the subject as she gestured toward their waitress for the bill. "I need to go confirm my flower order. Do you want to come with me?"

Tingin dropped his paper napkin to the table and shook his head. "I think I'll pass, but give me a call when you go for the menu tasting!"

* * *

Tierra was still annoyed with her brother as she headed in the direction of McKinney Avenue and the Timeless Fiori floral shop. Her appointment with Hilary, the head designer, had been a last-minute scheduling, and Tierra didn't like that she was feeling out of sorts when the moment should have been one of her happiest. She heaved a deep sigh. *Why aren't I happy?* she wondered.

Tierra had always been certain that she would one day be Mrs. Damien Porter. She'd been convinced ever since she'd laid eyes on the boy the day she and her brother had moved into their grandmother's north Dallas home, just two doors down from where Damien lived. The two had both been twelve years old.

The term *rocky* didn't begin to define their relationship. For as long as Tierra could remember, she'd been enamored with Damien, and more times than she cared to count, Damien had been enamored with someone else. All through school Damien had been attentive and caring, but his attention could too easily be diverted elsewhere. Their high school cheerleading team had given Tierra a real run for her money, but despite his many trysts, their friendship had always drawn Damien back to her side.

College had proven to be the turning point in their youthful infatuation. Her senior year at Texas Southern University and her interest in the TSU Tigers' star quarterback had pricked Damien's jealous streak, and that quarterback's interest in Tierra had finally motivated him to make a commitment to her. He had professed his adoration for her, and the two had been virtually inseparable from that moment on.

His proposal had come five years ago, just after Damien had enlisted in the military. But the engagement had been an extended one since Damien hadn't felt it necessary for them to jump right into anything. Then with his recent deployment to Afghanistan they'd been hesitant to officially set a date. But now he was expected back for a little rest and relaxation, and the two intended to tie the knot while he was home on extended leave. Meanwhile, Tierra had been left with the mechanics of putting together a wedding all by her lonesome.

Now with the plans for her dream wedding coming together, albeit slowly, her brother had to spoil the fun by reminding her once again that no one—not him, their grandmother or her few friends—were actually happy about her marrying Damien. Every one of them believed the man couldn't be trusted to honor her love by being forever faithful. But Tierra trusted that once they were husband and wife the two of them would prove everybody wrong. She heaved another deep sigh. She still couldn't shake the melancholy that had gotten a hold of her.

She forced herself to smile. Damien would be home in less than thirty-six hours, and then the last pieces of her life plan would all fall into place. Determined to kick her excitement into gear, she accelerated the vehicle, exceeding the posted speed limit. If nothing else, Tierra couldn't wait to get to her future. She was a young woman who couldn't wait to be a wife.

Chapter 2

Staff Sergeant Travis Stallion drew two fingers around the collar of his military dress shirt, anxious to lose the necktie and formal uniform. He would have given anything to have traveled home in his combat uniform, the casual, camouflage-colored attire far more comfortable, but he was representing the United States Army, and his dress greens were mandated.

As he threw his hand in the air, gesturing for a taxicab, he was counting down the minutes when he could pack away everything military and don his favorite jeans and white T-shirt. But he had one more stop on his list of things to do before he could officially begin his leave and simply relax for the next thirty days.

Stepping inside the yellow cab that had stopped in front of him, he leaned back against the vinyl seats and closed his eyes, purposely avoiding the conversation the young taxi driver was trying to have with him. He was too tired from his travels to talk, so he pretended to sleep to avoid the polite chitchat.

As the driver finally focused on maneuvering the car through the heavy traffic, Travis tapped his hand against his heart and the many mounted ribbons that adorned his chest. Confirming that he still had possession of the sealed envelope he'd placed in the inside pocket of his green dress coat, he took a deep breath, then slowly blew warm air past his full lips.

He'd given Private First Class Damien Porter his solemn word that he would deliver that sealed envelope to Porter's girl, who lived in Dallas, where he would be staying for the next thirty days. The young woman's downtown address would be his last stop before he found his way to his own family's home for the month.

As the taxi pulled up in front of the Main Street address and the high-rise apartment building, Travis asked the driver to wait for him to return.

"Just keep the meter running," he said as he exited the cab. "This shouldn't take long at all."

The taxi driver nodded, settling back in his seat to wait.

As Travis stood on the sidewalk, taking in his surroundings, he was impressed with the location. The neighborhood was an upscale one, and be somewhere he could eventually see himself living, he thought. He was just steps away from Neiman Marcus, the Urban Market Grocery and Café and the Main Street entertainment district, and he was in walking distance to the Arts District and Victory Park.

Inside the building he was greeted warmly by the building's concierge.

"Good afternoon, sir. How may I help you?"

Travis nodded with a quick flick of his head. A faint smile pulled at his mouth. "I'm here to see Miss Tierra Braddy, please. My name is Travis Stallion."

"Yes, sir. I'll let her know you're here," the man said as he reached for the telephone resting atop the marbled desk.

After a brief exchange, he pointed Travis to the elevators. Before the soldier could step inside, the man called out to him. "Excuse me, sir, I just wanted to say thank you." He gave Travis a quick wave of his hand. "We really appreciate the armed forces and what you men are doing for us over there."

Nodding his gratitude, Travis allowed the doors to close shut between them. Seconds later the conveyor stopped on the twenty-second floor. Heading down the carpeted hallway, he made his way to the young woman who stood waiting in her doorway, intrigue painting her expression as she watched him approach.

"Hi," Tierra said excitedly, extending her hand in greeting. "It's a pleasure to meet you, Staff Sergeant Stallion. Damien has told me so much about you."

And Damien had, extolling the man's many virtues in every conversation the two had ever had. Her fiancé had been in awe of his thirty-one-year-old platoon leader, holding the man in high esteem. His descriptions, though, didn't do the handsome man justice. Tierra was surprised by the smoldering stare that was eyeing her so intently. His pale, almond-shaped eyes seemed to draw her in like a moth to a flame. Tierra was slightly surprised by their intensity, and her reaction. She tried to shake the sensation from her thoughts.

Taken aback by the vibrant smile washing over him, Travis was briefly stunned himself. He hadn't expected the woman to be so extraordinarily beautiful. But beautiful she was, with her deep brown eyes, caramel candy complexion and a full luscious pout a man could imagine himself kissing. Tierra Braddy was probably the most exquisite creature he had ever laid his eyes upon. A flood of electric energy surged through his spirit.

Travis was suddenly aware of her small hands clasping tightly to his own large appendage. His gaze fell to the perfectly manicured fingers that warmly caressed the back of his own hand, then rose back to the woman's smiling face. The moment was strangely surreal, feeling as though it were playing out in slow motion. His tongue suddenly felt too big for his mouth, words caught deep in his chest.

So focused on her own rising anxiety, Tierra didn't seem to notice Travis's sudden discomfort. Fighting to stay focused, she eagerly pulled him inside, closing the door tightly behind them as she chatted nonstop.

"This is such a surprise. Damien didn't tell me you were coming stateside. Where is he? Did you two travel back together? I'm so excited to meet you!"

"It's a pleasure to meet you, too, Ms. Braddy," he finally managed to mutter, his voice sounding foreign to his own ears. "Please, call me Travis."

She repeated her questions.

"No, ma'am, we didn't. That's why I'm here. Private First Class Porter asked me to personally deliver this to you," he said, reaching inside his breast pocket for the letter that had traveled home with him.

Travis forced himself to continue. "He stressed

that it was very important you receive it as soon as possible."

The look of fear that crossed the woman's face suddenly tore at his heartstrings as she took the envelope from his fingers, her own hand shaking ever so slightly. Her confused stare met his.

"There's nothing wrong with him, is there?" she asked, a rise of distress spilling into her tone. "Damien's okay, isn't he?"

Travis nodded. "When I last saw him he was doing just fine."

Tierra exhaled a deep sigh of relief, pulling the letter to her chest. "You scared me," she said, her voice dropping a few octaves.

"I'm sorry, I didn't mean to," Travis responded. He took a step toward her, the move unconscious as he suddenly wanted to pull her into his arms to ease the nervous edge that had gripped her spirit. "I really didn't mean to upset you."

Tierra giggled softly, mildly embarrassed. "I'm fine," she said, brushing her palm against his forearm. "I'm also very rude. I haven't even offered you anything to drink. Can I get you something, Travis?"

"No, but thank you for offering. Unfortunately, I really have to be going," the man said, moving back in the direction of the door. "My taxi is waiting for me downstairs."

"But you'll come back? Right?" Tierra asked, the words slipping past her full lips before she could stop them. She stammered ever so slightly. "I…I mean, when Damien gets here tomorrow. You'll come back and have dinner with us, and you'll come to the wedding, I hope?"

That brilliant smile washed over him a second time. Travis suddenly felt like a match had ignited him on fire. He would have given anything for a cool wave of air to still the heat that had rushed from his head to his feet. "Certainly," he muttered softly, trying to ignore an obvious wave of jealousy that was washing over him. "I look forward to it," he said, the polite fib rolling like butter off his tongue.

"Thank you for stopping by," Tierra said. "I know Damien really appreciates everything you've done for him. And this—" She gestured with the sealed mailer. "This was truly above and beyond your call of duty."

Nodding his head, Travis excused himself, then stepped into the hallway. As the door closed behind him, he suddenly couldn't help but wonder what had been secured inside the envelope he'd just delivered.

Locking the door behind her unexpected guest, Tierra moved from her foyer to the large windows that looked out to the lighted ball atop Reunion Tower and the neighboring Bank of America building. The stunning views had been a key selling point when she had searched for her first home. But Damien hadn't been impressed.

Damien hadn't wanted her to invest any of the money she'd inherited from her late grandfather into a home. The man had had a million get-rich-quick schemes that he thought would be more fruitful. But Tierra had erred on the side of caution, seeking out her grandmother's advice and advice from the attorney who'd been hired to oversee the small fortune she and her brother had been blessed with. The security of real estate had proven to be exactly what she'd needed, despite Damien not wanting to support her decision.

Sliding a manicured nail beneath the sealed flap, Tierra tore open the envelope, anxious to read what was inside. She smiled to herself, hoping the sweet words Damien had written to pave his way home would endear him to their friends and family.

Pulling the neatly printed note from inside, she read it once, twice and then a third time. An hour later she was still reading it over and over again, the first of many tears streaming over the curve of her high-boned cheeks as she tried to make sense of the words that tore at her soul.

Chapter 3

The taxi driver, still trying to make small talk about the political issues currently in the headlines, pulled his taxi past the gated entrance of Briscoe Ranch, maneuvering the circular driveway to the front entrance of the large home. With a quick nod of gratitude, Travis pressed two twenty-dollar bills into the man's hand and made a quick escape from the backseat of the vehicle.

As Travis watched the car make its way back off the property, he turned around to take in his surroundings. Briscoe Ranch was well over eight hundred acres of working cattle ranch, an equestrian center and an entertainment complex that specialized in corporate and private client services. The ranch housed two 20,000 square-foot event barns and a country bed-and-breakfast. With the property being central to Austin, Houston, Dallas and Fort Worth, Briscoe Ranch had made quite a name for itself. Travis was duly impressed.

Turning back toward the steps and the front door, he grinned widely when it suddenly swung open and his cousins Matthew, Mark, Luke and John Stallion all came barreling down to greet him.

The noise and banter was reminiscent of when they'd all been under the age of ten racing from one end of their late grandparent's home to the other. Each and every summer the cousins would come together and play until they were all exhausted. Those had been some of the best times in their young lives.

Travis couldn't help but note the deep family resemblance. The four brothers were the spitting image of his uncle, their father, David Stallion, and David's brother Joseph, Travis's father. All the men boasted imposing statures, black-coffee complexions, chiseled jaw lines and charismatic smiles. That striking family resemblance had skipped Travis, with him inheriting his mother's café au lait complexion and her light hazel-green eyes. But even with their differences, side by side he and his kin looked like chocolate and vanilla reflections of each other.

"Yo, soldier boy!" Mark Stallion bellowed, wrapping the large man in a big bear hug.

Luke slapped his cousin's palm. "Travis, my man!"

"Isn't he pretty in his uniform." Matthew laughed, his tone teasing as he embraced his cousin.

"Exceptionally!" John responded, he and Travis shaking hands as they bumped shoulders. "Welcome home, family!"

"It's good to be back." Travis grinned. "And look at you guys! I see this good life has been treating you four very well," he said as he patted Mark's abdomen.

John laughed. "That's sympathy weight. Mark's wife is expecting a baby, and for every pound she gains, Mark is gaining five."

Mark flipped a finger at his older brother. "Maybe two, but definitely not five."

"When did you get married?" Travis said, surprise showing on his face. "Weren't you going to be a confirmed bachelor forever?"

The large black man laughed, his head shaking. "I was, but then I met Mitch. I just couldn't help myself. The woman just took my breath away," Mark exclaimed, joy shimmering in his eyes.

Travis nodded, the memory of his encounter with Tierra Braddy suddenly intruding on his thoughts. He could fully understand how a woman might take a man's breath away, because Tierra had clearly left him gasping for air. He turned his focus back to the conversation and his cousins, who were regaling him with info about Mark's mechanic wife and their whirlwind romance.

"My girl tamed this Stallion man big-time," Mark said, his laugh a deep rumble that flowed from his midsection.

Matthew shook his head in agreement. "Brother finally had to turn in his little black book. But you know how Mark is," he said with a roll of his eyes. "Once John does something, he has to go and do it, too. Just like when we were kids."

Travis locked eyes with John. "Your wife's not pregnant, too, is she?"

John shook his head vehemently. "Oh, heck no!"

A soft voice called down from the top of the steps. "Why do you say it like that, John Stallion?" Marah

Stallion asked, her arms crossed over her chest as she stared down at her husband and his brothers.

John's wide smile gleamed back at her. "I was just saying that we weren't pregnant, baby! I didn't say it like it was anything bad!"

Marah laughed, a wry smirk filling her face. "I bet you didn't! You better watch yourself, John Stallion. You know I don't play like that!" She turned her attention to their arriving guest. "Hey, Travis! Just leave those jokesters standing right there and come on inside here. We've been cooking all afternoon. I hope you're hungry."

Travis laughed as he tossed his duffle bag into Luke's arms. "I'm starved. How are you doing, Marah?" he queried as he made his way to the top of the steps, leaning to kiss the woman's cheek.

"I'm doing just fine. I know you must be good and tired after your trip."

"I am. A good meal, a hot shower and a few hours of sleep and I might actually feel normal again," Travis said with a wide smile.

Marah patted his back. "I think we can take care of that for you," she said. She glanced over her shoulder, her husband shaking his head.

"You better be on top of your game tonight, Mr. Stallion. I'm not going to forget that 'heck no' comment anytime soon."

John pretended to groan, still grinning as he and his brothers made their way behind Travis and Marah. "Don't be like that, baby," he said, his voice a low whine. "You know I didn't mean anything by it."

Marah giggled. "I don't know anything of the sort."

John leaned to kiss his wife's mouth as he wrapped an arm around her waist and pulled her close to him. "Let me make it up to you," he said, his voice dropping to a low whisper as he nuzzled his cheek against hers.

Travis laughed. "I can certainly see what marriage and this good life has done to you!"

The sumptuous midday meal had left Travis full and satisfied. Marah had piled his plate high with fried chicken, macaroni and cheese, collard greens, corn bread and peach cobbler and had supplied freshly brewed and sweetened tea. He'd eaten well and was still stuffed from the experience.

He stepped out of the shower, wrapping his muscular body in an oversize, plush white towel. A stark contrast to the rough army towels he'd been using, the soft cotton fabric felt luxurious against his skin. Travis closed his eyes, relishing the sensation. An image of Tierra Braddy suddenly flitted through his mind, and he couldn't help but imagine how she might feel in his arms, her body pressed tight against his naked flesh. The imagery sent a spark of heat straight to his southern hemisphere, causing every muscle in his body to tense with frustration.

Moving to the sink, Travis turned on the faucet and splashed his face with cold water. This was getting out of control. He had only met the woman for a brief moment, and here he was starting to fantasize about her. Besides that, she had a man, and chasing another man's woman was not something he would ever contemplate. It had just been way too long since he'd enjoyed some female companionship on an intimate level. He was suddenly acting as if he were fifteen again, when raging hormones controlled his male impulses. He needed to regain some serious control.

Moving back into the immaculately decorated guest bedroom, he dropped down onto the bed and lay his body back against the padded mattress. Before sleep quickly consumed him, he couldn't stop himself from thinking about the woman. And he couldn't help but wonder if, just maybe, Tierra Braddy might be thinking of him, as well.

"I'll bet he got himself a good laugh out of it," Tierra exclaimed loudly as she paced the floor from wall to wall. "I can just imagine what a fool he thought I was, me going on and on about the wedding and the whole time Damien wasn't planning to show up."

Tierra brushed her tears away with the back of her hand, smearing her mascara and the blush that highlighted her cheeks. The magnitude of her situation blanketed her spirit. "How could he do this to me!" she moaned sadly, dejection masking her face.

Eden Waller and her younger sister, Marla Baron, both shook their heads, clucking their tongues in sympathy. Eden leaned forward in her seat, meeting Tierra's teary gaze as she passed the yellow sheet of lined note paper back to her friend.

"Tea, sweetie, you know better than anyone how Damien is. He's hurt you before. You know he was capable of doing that to you and worse. The guy is scum."

Tierra tossed her hands up in frustration. "Not

Damien!" she wailed. "His sergeant... How could the man just drop news like that in my lap and walk away? He seemed so sweet. How could he do that to me?"

Eden stole a quick glance toward her sister, the two women exchanging a confused look between them.

"Are you sure he knew?" Marla asked. "I mean, do you think he read the letter?"

Tierra stomped to the other side of the room. "I don't know. But it doesn't matter. I'm sure he knew. I just find it hard to believe Damien didn't tell him what he was up to. You know how men are. They put their business out there more than women do."

Both Eden and Marla took a deep inhale of air at the same time, the two women sensing that nothing they could say would give their friend any comfort. Neither of them had been surprised when a hysterical Tierra had shown up at the ranch devastated by the Dear John letter her beloved fiancé had sent to her. No one expected much of anything from Damien. They'd tried for too many years to get Tierra to see that the love of her life wasn't a man worthy of her heart. Eden had said it best: men like Damien Porter were what bad sperm produced.

Marla rose from her seat, offering Tierra a tissue for her runny nose. She shook her head. "What can we do to help you, Tea?"

Tierra finally collapsed into a chair, the hurt of it all weighing her down. She, too, shook her head. She couldn't begin to fathom how anyone could do anything to make any of this well ever again. "I guess I won't be needing that chapel now," she muttered softly.

Eden tapped a comforting palm against Tierra's knee.

"Why don't you stay here at the ranch with us for a few days? Take some time away from your normal routine to get some perspective. Next week you might actually see that this was for the best. Better it happened now than later, Tierra."

Tierra briefly closed her eyes, tears pooling behind her eyelids. "You sound like my grandmother," she said, her voice barely a whisper. "She said the same thing."

Tierra's grandmother, Deloriann Braddy, had never been a woman who bit her tongue. Mama Dee had been saying loudly, and often, how she didn't support Tierra's decision to marry Damien. She also hadn't bit back her glee in learning the wedding was off. It was just as the old woman had predicted would happen. Damien had betrayed her.

Tierra nodded her head. "Are you sure it won't be any inconvenience? I just don't want to be alone in my apartment, and I'd rather live out of my car than go to my granny's and have her and Tingin say they told me so one more time."

Marla nodded. "It's no problem at all. You know we have a ton of space here, and right now the only other guest we have is John's cousin visiting for the month."

"John?" Tierra queried

"Our sister Marah's husband. I don't think you've met Marah yet, have you?" Marla responded.

Tierra shook her head. "Not yet." There was a moment of pause while Tierra contemplated what she should do. Finally, she answered, "Well, if you're sure it won't be a problem."

Eden wrapped her arms around Tierra's shoulders.

"We are. Come on. I'll show you where your room will be."

Following behind her friend, Tierra swiped at the tears that had begun to fall from her eyes for the umpteenth time. She hated that she couldn't stop crying, but it hurt to admit that she had been wrong. It hurt even more to think that after all this time Damien hadn't really cared about her at all.

At the top of the stairwell, Tierra turned to her friend and gave a sincere smile. "Eden, I really appreciate this."

Eden grinned. "Everything's going to be all right, Tea. Just keep believing that."

As Tierra turned back toward the hallway, she wasn't prepared for the large man who suddenly bounded from behind a closed door, stepping directly in front of her path. The duo slammed harshly into each other.

Instinctively, Travis reached out to grab the woman he'd just bowled over, intent on keeping her from falling to the floor. "I am so sorry," the man exclaimed, his voice echoing loudly around them.

"Ouch," Tierra muttered at the same time, gripping tight to the large arms that held her firmly by the shoulders. "Excuse me." She looked up into the man's face, recognition washing over her. "You!"

Travis's eyes widened with surprise. "Ms. Braddy!"

The couple stood staring for just a brief moment, then before she could stop herself, Tierra balled up a tight fist and slammed it hard into Travis Stallion's abdomen.

Chapter 4

Travis was still rubbing at his sore stomach muscles. Had he been expecting the slam into his solar plexus, it probably wouldn't have bothered him at all. But Tierra's punch had caught him completely off guard, and truth be told, for a little woman she packed one heck of a punch.

He still didn't have a clue what he had done to deserve being punched but figured by the way Tierra had run back down the length of stairs and out the front door that it had to have something to do with the letter he delivered.

Eden had only shrugged her shoulders before turning an about-face to go after the woman. The expression on her face was as shocked as his.

Making his way downstairs, Travis's curiosity was piqued. He was even more interested in knowing how Tierra had even known to find him there. Question after question raced through his thoughts as he stepped out onto the large porch.

The two women stood in front of the porch swing, Tierra sobbing uncontrollably. Her tears unnerved Travis and his usual steady and calm demeanor was suddenly anxious. Pushing both hands into the deep pockets of his jeans, Travis's steps forward were tentative, the man not wanting to intrude where he might not be wanted.

Eden acknowledged him first, her head shaking with concern. She patted Tierra gently on the shoulder, leaning to give her friend a quick hug before making a polite exit. As Eden moved past Travis, she leaned up to whisper into his ear.

"Go easy on her. She just had her heart broken."

Travis nodded ever so slightly. He took a quick glance over his shoulder as Eden stepped through the home's front door. The woman's stare back was equally curious as she looked from him to Tierra and back. She tossed him a quick smile of encouragement before disappearing inside. Turning his gaze toward Tierra, Travis didn't have a clue what to say or do. The woman's distress had knocked him completely off center.

Consumed with grief, Tierra didn't bother to acknowledge him. Dropping down onto the swing's cushioned seat, she dropped her head into her hands, swiping at the tears that didn't look like they'd be stopping anytime soon.

Travis took a deep breath, blowing warm air back out slowly. He moved to Tierra's side and took the seat beside her. Neither one said a word as they settled shoulder to shoulder against each other. Travis fought the urge to wrap his arms around her torso, sensing the gesture wouldn't be appreciated. He heaved another deep sigh.

Staring out over the landscape, Travis watched the comings and goings of the ranch hands as they went about their morning chores. Having forgotten his wristwatch in his room, he had no idea how long they'd been sitting there, but when the horses were being corralled to another pasture and his stomach was rumbling loudly for a morning meal, he figured it was as good a time as any to initiate a conversation. Tierra's sobs had finally slowed to a low sniffle, then suddenly she had a bad case of the hiccups.

Travis smiled sweetly. "Hold your breath. That might help."

Tierra cut a quick glance in his direction. "That never—" *hic* "—works," she muttered harshly.

There was a moment of pause before Travis said anything else. "Would you like me to get you a large glass of water?" he asked.

"I just want—" *hic* "—you to—" *hic* "—leave me alone," Tierra answered.

Travis moved to get up from his seat, but Tierra's next comment stopped him cold.

"I thought you—" *hic* "—were nice. Why—" *hic* "—would you do that—" *hic* "—to me? How—" *hic* "—could you?"

A look of confusion dropped over the man. Gripping her by her shoulders, Travis moved Tierra to face him. "How could I do what? I don't know what it is you're talking about, Tierra."

He felt her tense beneath his touch, her hands balling once again into tight fists, as she rose from the swing.

"At least tell me what it is you're mad about before you throw another punch," Travis said, "and don't take it personally if I punch back," he added, an amused smile pulling at his mouth.

Tierra met his deep gaze evenly, unsure if she wanted to laugh or start crying all over again. Feeling completely defeated, she collapsed back against the swing's cushions.

Travis was still eyeing her intensely. Tierra liked his eyes. She imagined a woman could easily lose herself in his eyes, if she were so inclined. Lost in his eyes a woman might imagine herself wrapped in his arms. In his arms, the possibilities that could be fathomed were endless. Tierra felt her breath catch deep in her chest as a flutter of something she didn't recognize flitted through the pit of her stomach. She shook the sensation away as quickly as it had risen.

Reaching into the pocket of her khaki slacks, Tierra pulled the dreaded letter from inside. Unfolding the tear-stained paper, she barely glanced down at it as she passed it over to Travis.

"Read it out loud," she said, her tone commanding.

Travis's gaze moved from her face to the notepaper in his hand. The soiled paper had begun to weather from handling, and the damp moisture of saline had begun to fade away the neatly printed writing. He pulled the document closer and began to read. As he did, moisture puddled in Tierra's dark gaze, threatening to spill over her cheeks again.

"Dear, Tierra. I hate to do this, but I know it's the best thing for us both. I won't be coming back to

Dallas. I can't marry you. I've met someone here who makes me very happy. I wish I could be the man you want me to be, Tierra, but I can't. I hope we can still be friends. I wish you all the best in the world. Damien Porter."

When he finished reading, Travis let the paper drop into his lap. Beside him, Tierra forced herself not to start crying all over again. She choked back a deep sob as she picked the letter up from where it had fallen and slowly tore it into shreds.

You could have warned me," she whispered softly. "What? Did you and Damien have a good laugh planning how you'd do it? I bet you can't wait to rush back and tell him how torn up I was so you two can bust a gut making a joke out of it all."

Travis was flabbergasted, astonishment registering on his face. He leaned forward, grasping both of Tierra's hands beneath his own. The torn shreds of paper fluttered down to the planked floor and across the perfectly manicured lawn.

"Tierra, I knew nothing about this. Private Porter never told me what he had written or what his plans were. The only thing he ever said was that it had to do with your wedding plans and that it was important it get to you as soon as possible. That's all. I swear. If I had known..." Travis hesitated. He couldn't begin to tell her what he would have done had he known. Suffice it to say, it would not have turned out well for Damien Porter.

Travis had been too nice, Tierra thought as she peered out the window to the landscape outside. She'd believed him when he'd said he didn't know anything about Damien's letter. She also sensed he would never have delivered news like that if he had been aware. Clearly the man was a gentleman who cared about her feelings.

Tierra blew a soft sigh past her glossed lips. In the distance she could see Travis interacting with his family as they all stood watching the horses being exercised in the corral. Tierra had been at the window watching him and the other men for some time.

He liked to laugh she noted, observing him as he threw back his head, chuckling heartily. The wealth of it seemed to rise from deep in his midsection, and Tierra imagined that with his deep baritone voice Travis's laugh could be a balm to a woman's ears. She couldn't help but hope that one day the two of them might find something to laugh about together.

She had left him sitting alone on the porch hours earlier, excusing herself to go wash her tear-streaked face and lie down for a nap. The man had still been holding both of her hands tightly beneath his own. Tierra caressed the back of her hand where his skin had touched hers. Her fingers and palm still tingled from the heat of his touch.

"This is ridiculous," Tierra suddenly spoke aloud, tearing herself from where she stood. She threw herself down against the bed, blowing a heavy sigh. She needed to be plotting revenge on Damien for hurting her, not thinking about some other man's touch. She desperately wanted to be fishing in her bag of tricks for some way to pay Damien back for the hurt of it all. But for whatever reason, Tierra couldn't stop thinking about Travis Stallion.

From where she stood in the front foyer, Tierra could see Marla, Eden and their kinfolk cutting up in the family room. The family was having themselves a good time, and Tierra didn't want to interrupt and spoil the fun with her bad mood.

Trying to escape without being seen or heard, she tiptoed across the polished wood floors toward the front door. Her name being called stopped her dead in her tracks before she could wrap her hand around the doorknob.

"Tierra?" Travis called a second time, coming up behind her. "Is everything okay?"

The young woman winced with frustration before turning around to face the man. "I'm fine, thank you," she said as she forced a slight smile. "I just have some errands I need to run." Tierra turned back to the door, opening it widely as she hurried to make an exit.

Still moving close behind her, Travis followed her outside. "Do you mind if I tag along with you? I would really like to see some of Dallas if I can."

Moving forward, Tierra winced again. She wasn't in the mood for company. "Maybe some other time, Sergeant Stallion. Right now I would just really like to be alone," she said as she reached her car. "The peace and quiet will be good for me."

"Maybe so," Travis stated, pulling open her passenger-side door. "But I think being with friends would be better for you right now," he said, a wide grin filling his handsome face. "You won't even know I'm here, friend."

Before she could respond, Travis stepped into her Saturn roadster and settled down comfortably in the front passenger seat. It was clear that nothing Tierra could say or do would be able to change his mind. She decided not to say anything at all, hoping the look she gave him would be enough to express her displeasure. She slid into the driver's seat and started the engine.

"So, what kind of music do you like to listen to?" Travis asked as he reached across her dashboard and turned on the car's stereo system. He began to scroll through the local radio stations.

Tierra cut her eyes in his direction. "How is this quiet?" she spat.

The man laughed, his disposition teasing. "Oh, you thought I was actually paying you some attention!"

A deep frown pulled at Tierra's mouth, aggravation clouding her expression. The man was hardly moved as he winked in her direction. Still smiling, Travis nodded his head as he settled back against the leather seats. His head bobbed in time with the music playing.

Tierra's own head shook at the absurdity. Shifting into drive, she pulled her car into the circular driveway and pulled away from the Stallion family home. As she navigated the traffic, the sound of jazz music settled comfortably between them.

The midday sun had settled nicely in the afternoon sky. The air was heated with just the hint of a breeze blowing. With the top down and the seductive tunes billowing from the speakers, the day could have been considered almost perfect.

Tierra suddenly wished she didn't feel so alone. Even with the gorgeous man seated beside her she was feeling like she didn't have a friend in the world. Heaving a deep sigh, Tierra stole a glance in Travis's direction. The man's gaze was fixed on the highway. His head bobbed and he patted his hand on his knee to the beat of the music.

He looked far more relaxed than he'd appeared the day before, his casual styling suiting him nicely. And just like the day before, the man was exceptionally attractive. His rugged good looks could make a woman lose her mind, Tierra thought, admiring the chiseled line of his features and the lush, full lips that pouted ever so slightly. Tierra couldn't help but wonder what kissing those lips might feel like.

She shook her head vehemently, appalled that just hours earlier she'd gotten her heart broken and here she was now, wondering what it might be like to kiss another man.

"You shouldn't have come," she suddenly said out loud, the words coming out of her mouth in a rush.

"Excuse me?" Travis said as he settled his intense stare on her.

Tierra's eyes flitted from the road to his face and back again. *Lord, have mercy,* Tierra thought. *Why does he have to look at me that way?*

She heaved another deep sigh, the air catching in her chest as she held her breath for a brief moment. She reached for the volume button on the car radio and turned it down until the music was barely audible. "I said you shouldn't have come. This was a bad idea."

Travis smiled, not bothering to respond. He turned the radio back up, his gaze still focused on the side of her face. He couldn't get over how incredibly beautiful she was. The woman was perfection personified. Private Porter had to have been a complete fool to let such an incredible creature get away.

His smile widened as the muscles in her face twitched with frustration. Without giving it any thought, he reached a large hand out and rested it on her shoulder. As he gently caressed the bare flesh, he felt her tense beneath his fingertips.

Tierra sucked in a deep inhale of oxygen. She hadn't expected the man to touch her, and suddenly the heat from his hand had ignited a fire deep in her midsection. It was all she could do to keep from running her car off the road.

"Hey, we're in this together now, so go with it. So, what are we doing? What's our first stop?" Travis asked, his hand still teasing her flesh as his fingertips tap danced against her skin.

Taking a second inhale of air, Tierra shifted her shoulder upward, rotating it away from the man's touch. "I have to go by the florist and cancel my flower order. In fact, I have to cancel everything I've ordered for the wedding. I don't know what you're doing."

"What kind of flowers did you order?" Travis asked nonchalantly, his gaze still piercing.

"What?"

"Tulips, sunflowers? What kind?"

Tierra chuckled softly, her head shaking at the absurdity. "What does it matter? I'm canceling them."

"Just curious," Travis said, his seductive smile returning. "I'm a rose man myself. I want to see my future wife walking down the aisle surrounded by a field of roses." He crossed his arms over his chest as he leaned back into the leather seat.

Tierra rolled her eyes skyward. "Bully for you," she said, thinking about the classic bouquet of pink and yellow tea roses that she had planned to carry, and the exquisite sprays of roses that were supposed to adorn the chapel and banquet hall.

Travis laughed warmly. "I was just saying."

As Tierra pulled into the parking lot of the flower shop, she shot him an evil look. "Well, don't," she said. "In fact, pretend you're not even here and we'll get along just fine."

As she stared in his direction, Travis met her gaze, allowing her eyes to linger with his for a second longer than necessary. Nodding his head slowly, he said nothing as he exited the car and moved quickly to the driver's-side door. Opening it widely, he extended his hand to help her up and out of her seat. As Tierra came to stand before him, his beautiful smile widened to a deep grin, pocketing full dimples in each cheek.

"So, really, did you pick roses?" he said. "Because I feel like you would be a rose kind of girl."

Chapter 5

Travis watched as Tierra stomped up the porch stairs and into the large home. Her vehicle was still vibrating from the harshly slammed door. A sly smile pulled at his mouth as he leaned against the car's fender, his arms crossed evenly over his chest. He laughed out loud, fully aware that Tierra was angry. And even though she was directing all that hostility in his direction, he understood that Tierra Braddy really wasn't angry with him.

The two had made three stops. The floral shop, Two Sisters Catering and the Warren Barrón Bridal Shop. With each stop, the shopkeepers had been extremely gracious after hearing that Tierra had essentially been abandoned at the altar.

It had taken some negotiating to get a refund of her deposit for the flowers, but the caterer had only to return the check Tierra had written just days earlier, their bookkeeper having yet to deposit it in the bank.

The experience at the dress shop, however, had been a whole other animal. The elderly woman who greeted her at the door had been excited to see Tierra, rushing to the back room for the Monique Lhuillier gown that was hidden beneath the protective dress bag.

Tierra's eyes had widened in horror, the large orbs misting with tears. Before the woman could think to unzip the bag and expose the dress, Tierra had begun to cry.

Travis had explained the situation as best he could as Tierra had stood there sobbing uncontrollably.

"I'm so sorry, dear!" the old woman had exclaimed, clucking her tongue and shaking her head.

"So you see," Travis continued, "Ms. Braddy needs to cancel her dress order."

"Oh, my!" The woman's facial expression changed. "I wish we could help you, but the dress is already here. As I explained when we placed your order, your gown is not returnable once it's delivered, and there can be no refunds."

"But what am I going to do with it?" Tierra finally gushed. "I don't need a wedding gown!"

Their sales clerk nodded her understanding. "You understood when you placed the order, Ms. Braddy, that all sales are final. Perhaps you can put it away and save it for a rainy day?"

"A rainy day!" Aghast, Tierra stared at the woman with dismay. "Are you out of your—"

Travis interjected. "I'm sure we'll be able to find another use for the thing," he said, trying to lighten the moment.

"It's not a *thing*," Tierra shouted. "It's my wedding gown! Do you even have a clue?"

Travis shrugged. "Can I see it?" he asked, gesturing to the sales woman to draw down the zipper.

Tierra's eyes widened in horror as she suddenly rushed between him and the gown. "You can't!" she exclaimed frantically. "You can't look at it."

"Why?" Travis's expression was curious.

"Because you're not supposed to see it before the wedding! A groom is supposed to see the bride's gown for the first time when she's walking down the aisle wearing it!"

Travis had raised a questioning eyebrow. A slight smile pulled at his mouth as his head nodded above his thick neck. "Whatever you say," he said softly. He took a step in Tierra's direction, wrapping his arms around her torso. For a split second he felt her body stiffen ever so slightly, and then she slumped against him in defeat, her forehead falling into his chest.

"I don't know why I'm mentioning that stupid custom. My wedding is off," she said, sobbing into his shirt. Over her shoulder, he nodded at the woman who was watching the two of them curiously.

"Thank you," he said. "If it won't be a problem, we'll come back later for the dress."

"No problem at all," the woman answered. "We have to do one more fitting, so whenever Ms. Braddy is ready just let us know."

Maneuvering the teary-eyed woman out the door and to her car, Travis helped her into the passenger seat, taking over behind the wheel. They'd probably traveled ten miles before Tierra's sobs had transitioned to dry heaves and stale air sighing through her lips. Another ten miles and the woman had grown completely quiet, staring off into the distance as she gnawed on her fingernails.

Travis heaved a very deep sigh, still staring into space after Tierra. She hadn't spoken one word to him on the ride home. But even as the two of them had ridden back across town in silence, Travis couldn't help but wonder just how exquisite Ms. Tierra Braddy might look in her dream wedding gown, walking down a chapel aisle in his direction.

After throwing the length of her body across the king-size bed, Tierra grabbed one of the plush pillows from beneath the bed's down comforter and pulled it to her chest. Rolling onto her side, she hugged the pillow as she drew her knees upward, curling her body tightly around its form.

She felt like crying again but didn't have any tears left to shed. And she simply refused to shed another drop for a man who hadn't been worth the time of day, let alone her love. If she cried again anytime soon it definitely wouldn't be for Damien Porter, she professed to herself.

Tierra squeezed the pillow tighter, digging her nails into the cotton fabric. She took a deep breath and then another, drawing as much air into her lungs as she could.

It was suddenly warmer than she would have liked it to be. She could still feel the heat from Travis Stallion's body against her own. The man had held her too close, his body feeling so good and so right against her own that Tierra was certain there had to be something seriously wrong with him doing it, and with her for having enjoyed it as much as she had.

"What is wrong with me?" Tierra questioned out loud. She rolled from one side to the other, conflicted by what she was feeling and what she thought she should be feeling. None of it was making an ounce of sense to her.

But she had thoroughly enjoyed being in that man's arms. He had held her and she had felt safe and secure, her heartache lifted by the sheer warmth of his touch. Right then, in that moment, she would have given almost anything to feel his arms around her one more time.

She hadn't wanted to enjoy anything about their time together, and she hadn't wanted to like Travis as much as she found herself liking him. Especially while she was trying so hard to be angry at her ex-fiancé. But Staff Sergeant Travis Stallion had incredible presence. Tierra liked how he commanded attention without an ounce of effort. He carried himself with an air of confidence that only a few men possessed.

He'd taken full control as they'd moved from bridal venue to bridal venue. Each time Tierra had fallen apart, pieces of her spirit unraveling at the counter in front of a sales clerk, Travis had picked her up and put her back together again. He'd done so without hesitation, knowing not a thing about her.

Tierra also liked that he was slightly cocky but not in an unflattering way. He was self-assured just enough that it couldn't be misinterpreted as arrogance. Tierra imagined that was what made him such an exceptional leader, the reason his soldiers looked up to him.

With no clue to how long she'd been lying there tossing and turning as she thought about Travis, Tierra couldn't shake the sensation of his hands gently stroking her back as his broad chest had easily kissed the curves of her torso. Even with his hands long gone, his touch still burned too hot for comfort. Tossing her legs off the side of the bed, Tierra lifted herself up and headed for the bathroom, desperately hoping a cold shower would wash the heat away.

The decadent smell of barbecued meat wafted through the late afternoon air. Travis took a deep breath as he moved past the large black smokers positioned on the home's rear patio. His cousin Luke; Luke's fiancée, Joanne Lake; his cousin Mark; and Mark's wife, Michelle, were debating the relevance of Facebook versus Twitter as a marketing tool. Travis hadn't bothered to throw in his two cents, personally having no preference for one over the other. They both kept him in contact with folks he needed to stay in touch with.

He'd been waiting for Tierra, hoping that she could move herself past her hurt and anger to join them, but there had been no sign of her. His patience had worn thin, and now he was just anxious to see and spend time with the exquisite woman.

Excusing himself, he moved from his cushioned seat, through the back door and into the home's kitchen. Sisters Eden, Marah and Marla were deftly navigating the room as they prepped potato salad, baked beans and pineapple upside-down cake to accompany the racks of ribs barbecuing outside.

"Hey!" Travis chimed cheerily. "Have any of you seen Ms. Braddy?"

Marah cut her eye at Marla, both women smiling slyly. They both shrugged, a low hum easing past Marah's lips.

Eden laughed. "No, we haven't. I think she's still in her room."

Travis eyed the three questioningly. "What's so funny?"

Eden smiled in response. "Nothing. Nothing at all. Why don't you run up and let her know that we're almost ready for dinner?"

Travis looked from one to the other, each of them avoiding his stare. As he moved to the door, Marah and Marla both burst out laughing.

"What?" Travis asked again, a befuddled look etched across his features.

Eden shrugged as the three answered in unison. "Nothing!"

Tossing his hands in the air, Travis headed up the stairs. Moving straight to the guest room door, he knocked loudly, calling out, "Tierra? Hey, it's me, Travis. Eden wanted you to know it's time to eat."

When there was no response, he knocked a second time. "Tierra?"

Becoming concerned when there was still no response, Travis slowly eased open the room's door, peering inside. Tierra was nowhere to be seen, but he could hear her voice coming from inside the adjoining bathroom. Tierra was singing loudly, an off-tune version of Beyoncé's latest hit echoing off the walls. Even as Travis stepped into the room, toward the sound of her voice, he knew he should probably turn around and retreat. But curiosity had gotten the best of him.

Stopping short in the doorway of the bathroom, Travis's eyes widened, a deep grin blossoming across his face. Tierra lay comfortably in a garden tub filled with warm water and lavender-scented bubble bath. Headphones plugged her ears as she lay with her eyes closed tightly, her hands at shoulder level as she snapped her fingers to the beat of the song playing on her iPod. Her legs were crossed at the ankles, her feet propped against the tub's edge. It was the first time since they'd met that she seemed totally and completely relaxed.

Travis couldn't help but marvel at the sight of her lying there in all her glory. Even after holding her in his arms, Travis was still amazed at just how tiny a woman she was, her size 2 frame looking even smaller.

Her face shimmered with warmth, the steam from the hot water heating her caramel-colored complexion a rosy red. Her luscious, dark brown tresses were pinned atop her head, a few wispy strands framing her delicate face. She was stunning.

Snow-white bubbles danced atop the water's surface, the occasional breaks in their flow allowing him a quick peek at her form. Small, apple-size breasts bobbed at water level. If he hadn't been searching he would have missed the small heart-shaped tattoo that adorned the inner curve of her right one, the image as tiny and as petite as the rest of her. Her hardened nipples stood at full attention, bubbles and water caressing them easily.

Travis suddenly wanted to nuzzle his head against her chest to taste the chocolate delights. A quiver of heat surged through his groin and he felt himself lengthen in his jeans. He inhaled swiftly, fighting to stall the sensation.

When she pulled the short length of her legs toward her chest, then eased them back beneath the water, Travis knew he was completely enraptured. He could have stood there staring at her forever.

Shaking the reverie from his head, he eased back out of the room. He paused a quick minute, then cleared his voice and knocked gently on the door frame, calling out Tierra's name. Startled, Tierra jumped, water splashing onto the floor. "Who? What the…? Don't you knock?" she sputtered as she realized he was standing right outside the opened door.

"I'm sorry," Travis interjected. "You couldn't hear me, and I was trying to get your attention. Eden wanted me to tell you that dinner is ready." The man was still grinning broadly, his face hidden from her view.

Tierra reached for one of the large plush towels hanging from the towel rack. Drawing it up and around her body, she moved to shield herself from sight. "You really have some nerve," she said as she stepped out of the tub. Pressing her body against the bathroom wall, she peered around the door frame to where he stood, eyeing the man from head to toe.

Travis leaned back against the wall between them, his arms crossing evenly over his chest. He stared back. "So, are you coming down to dinner?" He smiled sweetly.

"You really need to get out of my room," Tierra responded. "I don't remember inviting you in."

"I just wanted to make sure you eat something. You're going to need your nourishment."

"Why?"

"Because, we've got a busy schedule this week, you and I."

"I don't remember saying I was planning to spend any time with you."

Travis laughed. "You didn't, but you are."

Tierra rolled her eyes skyward. "Why?"

"Because you like me," Travis answered smugly. He winked at her as he crossed back to the other side of the room.

"You really are an arrogant, annoying, pain in the butt," Tierra said, her head shaking.

Travis laughed. "I was just thinking the same thing about you."

"Get out!" She clutched her towel closer around her body.

Wrapping his hand around the doorknob, he paused. "Oh," he said staring back at her. "Really cute tattoo! It suits you."

Her eyes widening, Tierra screamed at the top of her lungs, "Get out!"

Chapter 6

There was no denying the strain between Tierra and Travis when the woman finally joined the gathering for dinner. The tension swelled so thick and full that you could have sawed it into pieces and played a game of hockey with them.

Tierra moved into the room and purposely avoided meeting the man's intense gaze. And he was staring, a quirky smile plastered across his handsome face. As she cast a sidelong glance in his direction, she was tempted to slap that smile away. She couldn't believe he had peeked into the bathroom and had seen her naked. *And just how long had he been standing there staring at me?* she wondered silently. *Too long!* Tierra thought, shaking her head. *Much too long!* She couldn't believe the man's audacity.

And she couldn't believe that she was excited at the thought of him. Even now, trying to reason with her own senses, she couldn't stop the quivering that had started in her feminine spirit and had spread throughout her whole body. She found herself yearning for his touch, and just the thought of his hands had her pulse beating like a steel drum between her legs.

He had beautiful hands. It was clear that he didn't neglect them, his nails clean and neatly manicured. His touch was strong but gentle, the large appendages belying the hint of calluses across his palms from the manual labor he did.

Tierra couldn't help but imagine his fingers dancing across her skin, tracing easy lines as he gently caressed her. She couldn't stop herself from imagining what it might be like to have him trace the line of her tattoo as his palm cupped the wealth of her breast. Tierra inhaled swiftly.

"Tierra?…Tierra? Are you okay?"

Her name ringing in her ears drew her back to the moment. "Excuse me? Oh, I'm sorry. I was just…"

Everyone seated at the table chuckled softly. "You were gone, girl!" Luke Stallion chimed.

"I want some of whatever you're having," Marah laughed.

"Excuse me," Tierra said, her gaze skating around the table. "I don't understand."

Eden patted her friend on the shoulder. "You were moaning, girl!"

Tierra's shocked expression made them all laugh a second time. "I was not!"

Marla nodded her head. "Well, it sounded like a moan, and the look on your face said whatever you were thinking about was good. Real good."

"Or *whoever* you were thinking about..." Eden added, her eyes moving in Travis's direction. The man grinned broadly.

Tierra blushed profusely, the temperature in the room suddenly uncomfortable. "I'm sure I didn't moan," she insisted, rolling her eyes and trying to laugh the moment away. "I was just thinking about the chores I finished today. If anything, I probably groaned," she said, desperate to change the subject.

"So, where did you two disappear to today?" Marla asked, looking from one to the other.

Tierra met Travis's gaze for the first time since they'd sat down for dinner. Her look was pleading.

Travis winked and smiled warmly. "Nowhere special," he answered, turning his attention back to Marla. "Tierra just gave me a quick tour of Dallas. Isn't that right, Tierra?' He met her gaze a second time.

The young woman nodded. "Yeah," she muttered softly, her eyes still locked with his. She was grateful that he didn't mention where they'd gone and what she'd had to do. She didn't want to start another conversation about her failed relationship. Gratitude spilled from her stare as she gave him a soft smile back, her mouth curling ever so slightly. Travis smiled again before breaking their eye connection when he turned to ask his cousin a question.

Conversation filled the room as the group chatted comfortably back and forth. As they enjoyed their dessert, Travis listened intently as Tierra discussed the nuances of preschoolers and kindergarten with a very pregnant Michelle Stallion. Mark and his wife were excited at the prospect of nurturing a newborn.

As she talked about her profession, Travis could see that Tierra truly loved what she did. She had always wanted to be a teacher, and from what he was hearing she'd known she'd wanted to teach students in the elementary school level from the very first day of her student teaching assignment. She'd been teaching kindergarten for five years since then, and clearly it suited her personality.

"Doesn't sound much different from what you do, Travis," Matthew said jokingly.

Travis laughed. "Except I get my kids from boot camp to graduation in twelve weeks," the man responded.

"Do you like being in the military?" Tierra questioned, curious to know more about the man.

Travis nodded. "I do. I enlisted right out of high school, and it was the best thing for me. It gave me discipline and guidance and allowed me to set goals for myself that I hadn't known possible. I also consider it an honor and a privilege to be serving my country."

Tierra smiled. "That's nice."

Everyone in the room paused, seeming to eye them both curiously. Eden broke the silence. "Tierra, have you seen our rose garden? It is absolutely incredible this time of year. Travis, why don't you walk Tierra down to the gardens and show her the blooms," she said, her tone just shy of commanding.

Travis eagerly set his wineglass on the table. "I'd be delighted. Ms. Braddy, would you care to join me?"

Marla pushed her gently. "She'd love to," she answered firmly.

Tierra tossed her friend an annoyed look. "I really don't think—" she started before Travis interrupted her.

"I promise," he said, rising to his feet, "I won't bite!"

Tierra sighed, moving to join him. As the two made their way out of the room, she muttered under her breath, "It wasn't you I was worried about."

The word *incredible* didn't begin to describe the luxurious grounds outside the family's home. The gardens were a classic formal display of beds of roses arranged in a grass-girded oval around an exquisite marble fountain. Thousands of plantings and dozens of varieties decorated the landscape, and the sweet aroma wafting through the warm evening air was pure decadence.

Tierra was awed by the sheer beauty of it all, her eyes wide with surprise. "Oh, my," she muttered softly as the two of them meandered slowly down one of the brick paths.

"Yeah, it's something," Travis said in agreement.

Without giving it any thought, he reached for her hand, entwining his fingers with hers. Tierra tensed ever so slightly, but she didn't pull away, allowing him to hold her hand in his. That simple gesture made his heart race, his cellular clock skipping multiple beats.

Tight-lipped, Tierra continued to walk in silence, completely overwhelmed by how comfortable it felt to be so near the man. As he chattered away about absolutely nothing, trying to draw her into conversation, she found herself amused by his efforts. It didn't take long before she finally allowed herself to relax and enjoy the moment.

"Do you always talk so much?" she questioned, a smug smile crossing her face.

Travis laughed. "Only when I have to answer my own questions. This conversation thing actually works better when the other person talks also. You might want to try it."

Tierra chuckled. "You really are full of yourself, aren't you?"

Travis shrugged his broad shoulders. "I'd call it confident."

"Have you always been this way?"

"No. Actually, I was exceptionally shy as a boy. Getting me to talk was like pulling teeth."

She nodded her head ever so slightly. "And who do we have to thank for your transformation?"

"The United States Army, ma'am!"

Tierra giggled warmly. "So that's what they mean when they say you can be all you can be. Interesting."

"Not really," Travis said, cutting his eyes at her. He changed the subject. "So, tell me more about you. I couldn't help but eavesdrop when you were talking about your job. You really love teaching, don't you?"

Tierra's face lit up, energy gleaming from her eyes. "I do. I love knowing that what I do might make a difference in their young lives."

Spying an empty bench nestled deep in the center of the garden, Travis pulled her along gently, guiding her to take a seat beside him. Turning his body to face hers, he rested his elbow along the back of the seat and his hand against the side of his head. "Now that's interesting. Tell me more."

Pulling both her knees to her chest, Tierra wrapped

her arms around her legs, her chin resting atop her knees. "I could get used to this," she said softly, her gaze skating across the wealth of color that decorated their view. "It's so pretty here."

Travis nodded but said nothing, his own stare focused on the woman's beautiful face as she continued to talk about herself. As Tierra drew him in, describing the sense of accomplishment she felt teaching children the basics of reading, writing and arithmetic, he was taken aback by the sheer enthusiasm expressed in her tone. He suddenly found himself asking her question after question, marveling at her answers and the passion she exuded.

"Doesn't that take up a lot of your time?" he questioned, as Tierra detailed the student advocacy program she'd initiated to help parents of children who were considered at risk.

"It does, but it's necessary. So many of these mothers are just children themselves. Many of them barely made it out of school, and suddenly they're faced with dealing with the same school administrators who had them as students. A few are intimidated by the whole process. What my program does is match a parent and her child with a mentor who is willing to attend parent-teacher conferences and serve as an advocate for that child and the family."

"It sounds like a lot of hand holding."

Tierra nodded, her wistful look suddenly pulling at Travis's heartstrings. "Sometimes, we need someone to hold our hand to help us get through those rough times."

"Yes, we do," he responded softly, his deep gaze melding with hers.

There was no denying the attraction he felt for her. Being with Tierra felt like the most natural thing in the world for him to do. He thoroughly enjoyed her company even when one of her mood swings had her defensive and difficult.

The wealth of emotion that had suddenly consumed him was unsettling, like nothing the man had ever experienced before. He liked her. He liked her more than he was willing to admit to himself, her energy so nourishing that his own spirit was soaring sky high. Travis suddenly realized that there was a four-letter word for what he was feeling, but he couldn't fathom himself using it to describe the intense emotion.

Tierra smiled sweetly as she turned her head to stare at the landscape surrounding them. For a brief moment, Travis was tempted to lean in for a kiss, but he stopped himself, biting down against his bottom lip to quell the longing. Restraint was difficult because he suddenly wanted the woman more than any woman ever before. But this was different, not just lustful desire pulling at him, but something else he'd never known before having wrapped a death grip around his heart.

Tierra Braddy was like an intricate present he was privileged to unwrap. There were layers and layers to her personality, each one revealing her vulnerabilities and her immense strength. She was compassionate, spirited and sensitive. There was also an aura of innocence about her that he found wholeheartedly refreshing.

Above them, the sky had darkened, nightfall coming

quickly. Before either realized it, they were lingering beneath the glow of a half moon and the incandescent outdoor lights, conversation still raining between them.

"It's getting late," Tierra said, casting a glance over her shoulder. "They've turned off the lights inside the house."

Travis looked down to his watch. "Would you believe it's almost two o'clock?"

"In the morning?" Tierra exclaimed, her shocked expression moving him to laugh.

"Yes, ma'am."

She shook her head. "You're bringing me into some really bad habits, Sergeant Stallion. It's well past my curfew, and I need my beauty sleep."

"It's a good thing you don't need much then, isn't it?"

Tierra smiled, pretending to be amused by his sense of humor.

"I've had a very nice time, Travis. Thank you."

"So did I, Tierra. I look forward to doing it again." The man's deep smile warmed her, his eyes dazzling with light.

Rising from her seat, she hesitated momentarily as Travis stood with her, taking a step in her direction until they were practically toe-to-toe.

"Do you really have to say good-night?" he asked, reaching for her hand one last time. His fingers gently caressed the center of her palm.

Tierra nodded, suddenly taken aback by his touch. She was flush with heat, her breathing coming in short gasps as she sucked in air. The temperature felt like it had risen tenfold. She took two steps back, widening the space between them.

"Sweet dreams, Travis," she muttered softly as she excused herself. Fighting not to look back, Tierra almost broke out into a full gallop as she retired to her room for the night.

Travis's stomach was aflutter with anxiety as he stared after her, sweat beading across his brow. It had taken everything in him not to follow behind her.

Hours later the house was still, quiet wafting through each room. Travis sat alone in the family's posh library. As he reclined in the leather executive's chair, he twirled a tumbler filled with cognac between both palms. Inhaling the rich aroma of the copper-colored liqueur, he was reminded of buttered toffee, anise and dried fruit. He chuckled softly to himself, thinking about the cheap, locally brewed beer he'd been sipping on just weeks earlier, one of the few times he and his men had been off duty and able to steal away for a few hours of rest and relaxation. It didn't compare to the expensive drink he was now sipping.

He hadn't wanted the night to end, and now, unable to sleep, all he could do was fantasize about him and Tierra being together. As they had stood together on the terrace, what he had wanted most to do was sweep Tierra up in his arms, carry her upstairs to one of the empty bedrooms, lay her across a king-size bed and make sweet love to her.

The time the two had shared had heightened every one of his senses, and as his thoughts ran back to her naked form reclined in the bathtub, blood surged through his groin, lengthening a rock-hard erection in his pants. He gulped the remainder of his drink, palmed his crotch and blew a deep sigh.

Tierra pulled a pillow between her legs, pressing her knees tightly together. After two cold showers she still couldn't stall the throbbing that was pounding at the cusp of her genitalia. The pulsation was vibrating throughout her entire body, quivering up through her abdomen to the top of her head and down her limbs, curling her toes.

By the time she'd made it back to her room, locking the door behind her, she'd been a complete and total mess. She couldn't understand why she was reacting so wantonly to a man she barely knew. But every time she was near Travis Stallion she wanted him, and not just for a few minutes of casual conversation. It had taken everything in her not to pull the man in behind her, leading him to her room for a private, one-on-one tête-à-tête. She would have opened herself to him willingly, her desire for the man so intense that it was all she could do not to implode from the heat of his touch.

And he had touched her, holding tight to her hand as his fingers had caressed her own. As they'd walked through the magnificent gardens her shoulder had pressed against his arm, bare flesh touching bare flesh. Even in the innocence of the moment, it had been the most erotic thing she'd ever experienced.

They'd bantered back and forth easily, and, watching him as he spoke, Tierra had become enamored with his mouth. Travis had the most beautiful mouth, she thought as her mind floated to the image of his full, succulent lips. With each word that he'd spoken she'd been focused on the line of his mouth, the curve of his lips, his perfect, snow-white teeth with their slight gap and the length of tongue that would occasionally slide like silk over marble when he licked his lips.

She had wanted nothing more than to be able to kiss his sweet mouth, and she'd even allowed herself to imagine those lips caressing every square inch of her body. Tierra heaved a deep sigh, rolling from one side of the bed to the other.

She would have given anything to ease the heat that was trying to consume her. Tossing the pillow aside, Tierra rose from the bed and moved to the window to stare out into the darkened night. She desperately wanted to believe that fantasizing about her and that man really wasn't such a bad thing after all.

Chapter 7

When Tierra woke the next morning, the sky was overcast, the hint of rain billowing through the early morning air. She pulled the cotton sheet up and over her naked body, tucking it beneath her chin. She'd cast off every stitch of her clothing in the night. Her tank top had been thrown across the foot of the bed just after midnight. Her satin sleeping shorts had been abandoned on the floor at three o'clock in the morning. She didn't have a clue when she'd slid out of her panties or even where they might be.

All she could remember was dreams of Travis Stallion haunting her sleep most of the night. She rolled onto her side, drawing her knees close to her chest.

She didn't have a clue what she planned to do for the day. If she had her choice, she wouldn't bother to get out of bed at all. But Travis had made it clear that whatever she'd be doing he planned to do it with her. She didn't imagine that inviting Travis into her bed for the day would be a good idea. *Then again,* she pondered, a slight smirk pulling at her mouth.

Just as she was imagining the possibilities, there was a knock on her bedroom door. Tierra could tell by the persistent rap that the person on the other side was anxious for her attention.

Standing out in the hallway Travis stood with his ear pressed to the door, listening for Tierra to respond. "Tierra, are you awake?"

"Go away, Travis!"

"Not until you let me in. Are you interested in some breakfast?"

"Excuse me?" Tierra leaned up in the bed, straining to hear the low tone echoing out in the hallway.

"I brought you some breakfast," Travis said, his voice chiming a little louder. "May I come in?"

"I don't think—"

Before she could get the words out, the door swung open. Travis stood in the entrance, a tray of breakfast foods balanced in one hand.

"Your eggs are getting cold," he stated matter-of-factly.

Her eyes widening, Tierra clutched the sheet tightly around her bare form. "What do you think you're doing?" Tierra quipped. "I'm not dressed yet!"

Travis shrugged. "Sorry, but I couldn't hear you."

Tierra inhaled sharply. "I'm not dressed yet," she repeated through clenched teeth.

Resting the tray on the nightstand, Travis plopped down onto the bed beside her. "So I see," he said as he passed her a white cloth napkin. "And since it's not often that I get to serve a woman breakfast in bed, we'll just ignore that indiscretion. I expect you'll do better next time."

Tierra shook her head in response to his bold words. "Look," she started, "This really isn't..."

Her voice trailed off. The words seemed to catch in her throat as Travis suddenly reached both of his arms around her torso to plump the pillows behind her back. As he leaned in close, the aroma of his cologne wafted past Tierra's nose. She inhaled swiftly, filling her lungs with the scent of him.

As he fluffed the pillow against her for support, his forearms grazed her bare shoulders. They both tensed, Travis's gaze melding with hers.

"Sorry about that," he muttered softly, drawing his body away from hers. He gestured with a quick nod. "Lean back and make yourself comfortable," he commanded as he reached for the wicker tray and sat it on her lap. He smiled sweetly.

"Bon appétit," he exclaimed as he pulled the silver lid from the plate.

The meal was an epicurean delight of scrambled eggs, thick bacon, pecan Danish and a bowl of fresh fruit. A large glass of sweetened pineapple juice and a single red rose completed the presentation.

Travis's flamboyant removal of the paper wrapper from a plastic drinking straw made her smile and seconds later, still clutching the bed sheet in front of her, she couldn't suppress the laugh that suddenly followed.

Hearing the deep chortle that rose from her midsection brought a wider grin to Travis's face. The sound was pure music to his ears, and he couldn't help but laugh with her. Reaching out a large hand, he touched her face, drawing his fingers along her profile. His thumb lightly caressed her cheek, and he was mesmerized by the downy softness of her skin. In that moment he would have given anything to cradle her in his arms and never let her go.

He'd known he was taking a chance when he'd pushed the door open before being invited inside, but he'd been anxious to see her. He'd barely slept, his dreams consumed with thoughts of her. And his instincts had told him that Tierra had really wanted to see him, too.

As she tried to hide her nakedness beneath the covers, he found himself enamored with the idea of the two of them together. The woman excited him like no other woman ever had before. And in that moment he was visibly excited. Needing a minute, he sat down in a chair that was next to the bed. He crossed one leg over the other to hide the fullness that had begun to swell hard in his jeans.

"This is crazy!" Tierra said, fighting the last of the giggles that had consumed her. "None of this makes an ounce of sense."

"It makes great sense. Now eat up, get dressed and be ready to rock and roll in thirty minutes. I'm anxious to get going. I'm sure we have lots to do today," Travis said as he came to his feet. "So figure out what it is we have to do today, okay?" He continued to smile down at her.

Tierra nodded. "I don't imagine you're going to let me say no, are you?"

"The word *no* is not in your vocabulary today, Ms.

Braddy." Travis moved back in the direction of the doo. He turned an about-face to stare at her, softly calling out her name. "Tierra."

"Yes?"

"You are incredibly beautiful when you wake up," he said, his eyes shining brightly. "Now, get a move on it. We will be leaving on time!"

As Tierra pulled her car onto the highway, a wide grin filled Travis's face. Cutting an eye in her direction, he reached for the radio. Tierra could tell by the look he tossed her that he was half expecting her to complain, but she refused to give him the satisfaction. The man was like a five-year-old as he depressed the buttons to find the perfect song. This time he chose a mix of reggae and Latin beats.

"So, what's on our agenda today?" Travis asked, finally leaning back in his seat. "Have we canceled the band?"

Tierra rolled her eyes skyward then refocused on the road, refusing to give him an answer.

"No band, huh? I didn't think so."

"What do you mean you didn't think so? Why wouldn't I have a band?" Tierra asked, annoyed with his tone.

Travis smiled. "I imagine you would have hired an orchestra for the ceremony. A few violins, some flutes, maybe a cello or two."

"You're so smug! Since you need to know so badly, we had a harpist, and I've already called her to cancel."

"A harpist! How did I guess?" A wide grin rolled

across his face a second time as he changed the subject. "So, where are we off to?"

This time Tierra smirked. "You wanted to ride shotgun, Sergeant, so ride. Today, you're going to get what you asked for."

Travis's eyebrows rose ever so slightly. "Should I be scared?"

The beautiful woman beside him chuckled warmly. "Now that's an understatement!"

Minutes later, Tierra pulled into the driveway of her grandmother's home. The small cottage was a welcome sight, with its bright arrangements of flora that decorated the landscape. Her grandmother's gardens were the pride of the neighborhood. Even beneath the graying sky, the saltbox architecture gleamed with light and warmth.

Deloriann Braddy was standing at her kitchen's sink when the two entered the immaculately decorated home. She was a robust woman dressed in a floral housecoat and satin bedroom slippers. From her large eyes and full cheeks down to her thick legs and wide ankles, everything about her was round in a pleasant, soft dough kind of way.

Her personality filled the room with a vibrant energy. The warmth she exuded was almost contrary to the new stainless-steel appliances and rich ebony color of the granite counter tops. Deloriann Braddy was more like the exterior of her home, with its brightly painted shutters, sweeping porches and massive floral beds, each conflicting with its newly redecorated interior. Tierra noted the look on Travis's face, reading his mind.

"My brother and I had it gutted last year. We gave her

new bathrooms and a chef's kitchen. She wouldn't let us change the home's footprint or the exterior, though."

The woman's gregarious voice boomed warmly. "Didn't need all these bells and whistles, but I can't tell you young people a thing. Y'all think you know it all." She turned to focus a curious eye on Travis, wiping her hands against a cotton dishcloth as she did.

"So, who's this young man?"

"Good morning, Mama Dee," Tierra said, reaching to kiss the woman's cheek. "This is Travis Stallion. Travis, this is my grandmother, Mrs. Deloriann Braddy."

"But everybody calls me Mama Dee," the matriarch said as she wrapped Travis in a large hug. "It's a pleasure, Mr. Stallion."

"The pleasure is all mine, ma'am, and please, call me Travis."

The woman paused briefly, still studying him before she responded, ignoring his request. "So, Mr. Stallion, how do you take your coffee?" Mama Dee asked, reaching for an empty mug and a freshly brewed pot of caffeine. "You do drink coffee?"

Travis smiled ever so slightly as he nodded his head. "Yes, ma'am. Cream and sugar, please."

"Sit down and make yourself comfortable, son," she said as she poured hot coffee in the cup she held in her hand and set it and a saucer down on the table in front of him. She pushed a container of milk and the sugar bowl toward him as she sat down with her own cup, sipping lightly at the hot fluid. "So, how do you and my granddaughter know each other?" Mama Dee asked.

Tierra smiled, pulling up her own chair to the table. "Travis is Damien's platoon leader," she said. "He came all the way to Dallas to tell me Damien didn't want to marry me."

Mama Dee laughed loudly. "You already knew that, granddaughter. Damien didn't need to send his boss to deliver that message."

Tierra rolled her eyes, a full pout pulling at her mouth. "Thank you, Mama Dee."

"It really wasn't like that," Travis said in his own defense. "I have family here in Dallas that I'm visiting while I'm on leave. Private Porter took advantage of my being here. I was an unwilling pawn and, unfortunately, although I didn't ask to be the bearer of bad news, it turns out that I was."

"Life doesn't always go as planned, Mr. Stallion, but you know that," Mama Dee said, her head bobbing against her thick neck. "Besides, look where it's brought you."

Travis's eyes met Tierra's. "Things happen for a reason, Mama Dee."

The older woman looked from one to the other, studying the two of them carefully as they continued to stare at each other, both seemingly oblivious to her being there. There was clearly something in the look they exchanged. Something the woman recognized but had never before seen in her granddaughter's expression. She suddenly had a ton of questions for the new man sitting at her kitchen table.

"Tierra, I need you to run that bag of clothes on the screened porch down to the church for me. Reverend is expecting it, and you can save me some time." She turned to Travis. "We've been collecting gently used clothing for the children. We've gotten some nice donations for families in need."

Tierra sighed. "Yes, Mama Dee. Travis and I will drop it off when we leave here."

"No, you can run them over there now. Have a conversation with Reverend about your situation while you're there. Ask him to say a prayer for you. Mr. Stallion can stay here and help me in the backyard," her grandmother commanded.

"But—" Tierra started to object, but the stern look her grandmother gave her stalled her words. She shook her head as she came to her feet.

Easing past Travis, Tierra leaned down to whisper into his ear. "Be afraid. Be very, very afraid!"

Chapter 8

As Travis and Mama Dee both enjoyed a second cup of java, the casual conversation had been like an easy calm before a storm. Collecting both cups from the table, Mama Dee rinsed them out in her sink, then carefully placed them in her new dishwasher. She gestured with a crooked finger for Travis to follow her out to the yard.

"It's a good day to be outside gardening," Travis noted as the old woman changed from her bedroom slippers into a pair of bright red rubber garden shoes.

Mama Dee nodded her silver-gray head in agreement as she plopped a wide-brimmed straw hat on top of her head. "A little more sunshine wouldn't hurt," she responded as she led him to the rear of her home.

Stepping out to the slate patio, Travis was taken aback by the wealth of plants that decorated the rear landscape. The yard was bordered by rich summer colors against dark green foliage, the textures creating a dramatic visual experience. The spectacular front yard paled in comparison.

"How beautiful," Travis muttered, his eyes skating back and forth as though he might miss something.

"This here is my sanctuary, Mr. Stallion. My home away from home."

"It's quite remarkable. I imagine it takes a lot of work."

Mama Dee nodded her head. "Tierra and her brother used to help. Tingin, that's Tierra's older brother, he still comes every now and again, but I can't remember the last time Miss Tierra got her hands dirty."

Travis chuckled. "Why doesn't that surprise me!"

Mama Dee gave him a curious stare. "So, what are your intentions, Mr. Stallion?"

"Excuse me? Ma'am, I'm not sure what you're asking me."

"I think you do. The question's not hard, chile'. What are your future intentions with my granddaughter?"

Travis suddenly felt like he was under a microscope, about to be exposed. "Well…ma'am…we're just getting to know each other. I'm hoping Tierra and I will be great friends."

"Just friends?"

"Well…I…" Travis stammered, his mind searching for an answer he thought she might be satisfied with.

Mama Dee fanned a gloved hand at him as she gestured for him to follow her with the wheelbarrow she'd just filled with supplies. She rested her gaze on him, and Travis knew that she was not a woman who would be easily satisfied.

"I see how you look at each other, Mr. Stallion. My

granddaughter has never looked at any man like she looks at you. You have her heart, and she doesn't even know it yet."

"I...don't...know..." Travis suddenly felt challenged, completely at a loss for words.

Mama Dee continued. "And I would venture to say that you're a bit smitten yourself, Mr. Stallion." The woman gave him a thoughtful stare.

Travis smiled. "It's not hard to see that your granddaughter is a very special woman, Mama Dee."

"Yes, Mr. Stallion, she is. And she's had her heart broken too many times by a man who didn't care about her. Damien played house with her emotions, stringing her along to make himself feel good. Tierra knew it, even though she tried to pretend that she didn't. She knew it, and she ignored it."

"And I'm sure when you pointed it out to her, she ignored you, too."

This time Mama Dee smiled brightly. "My granddaughter is as stubborn as a mule when she wants to be. Once she sets her mind on something, she'll dig her heels in and hang on tight."

Travis laughed softly. "I can see that about her."

"This is why I want to know your intentions. I don't want to see my baby girl heartbroken again."

Travis nodded his understanding. "I'd never do anything to hurt Tierra, Mama Dee."

"Never say never, Mr. Stallion. You don't know what you'll do until the situation presents itself. Now, tell me again, how long are you here for?"

"Just thirty days, ma'am. Then I have to go back to Afghanistan to finish my tour."

"And how long is that for?"

"I've only got eleven months left, unless, of course, I decided to reenlist."

"And is that something you might consider?"

The man paused, taking a quick minute to think about something he'd been thinking about since forever. "I consider myself a career soldier, Mama Dee. I haven't really given anything else any consideration."

"And now you have to," she declared, "as soon as you figure out your intentions with my granddaughter."

Travis reflected on her comments as Mama Dee began to hum, leaning to pull weeds from a designated spot in her garden. Time seemed to stand still as he thought back to the first time he'd laid eyes on Tierra, his heart skipping with excitement. He thought about the hurt he'd seen in her eyes when she talked about her ex-fiancé and their relationship. Then he reflected on what he saw when he'd been alone with her and she allowed herself to relax into the moment. There had been something else he'd seen in her haunting eyes.

As long as he could remember, Travis had been a man who dealt in facts. There were no gray areas in his life. Even as a little boy he'd lived by a code of honor that few others believed in. His enlisting in the military had been the answer to all of his prayers. Once he'd committed himself to Uncle Sam, there had never been time for a woman in his life, and definitely no woman he'd ever consider spending the rest of his life with. Then he met Tierra.

Just like that, it felt like everything he believed in and everything he had ever wanted changed. It had been love at first sight, and Travis hadn't believed it possible for him to love anything, or anyone, more than he loved the military. But he knew it, just like he knew his name. He loved Tierra Braddy, and the something else he'd seen in her eyes told him she might be feeling the same for him.

He inhaled deeply, his pulse racing ever so slightly. When Mama Dee's deep voice broke through the moment, he didn't have a clue how long he'd been standing there. Those few short minutes had felt like a lifetime.

"So, I'll ask you again, son. What are your intentions with my granddaughter?"

Travis met the matriarch's gaze and held it. He smiled, the wealth of it spanning across his face. Mama Dee smiled with him.

"With your permission, ma'am, I would really like to start dating your granddaughter. I think Tierra and I might be able to build something exceptionally special together, and I would really like to do whatever I have to do to make that happen. It would make me very happy if Tierra would give me a chance."

Mama Dee nodded her head slowly. "You've got your work cut out for you, Travis Stallion. But if my instincts are right, and they usually are, that might actually be possible. But we will just have to see, son. We will just have to see."

"I know it would be important to Tierra to have your support, Mama Dee. I hope you'll give me the opportunity to prove myself worthy of your granddaughter's love."

The old woman tossed him a warm smile, turning to stare into his eyes. "Someone certainly raised you right, son. I like how you do things." Pausing, she waved a hand in front of her face, swiping at the rise of perspiration that dampened her brow. Her head nodded ever so slightly above her round neck as she continued. "Tierra cares about you, Travis. More than she realizes. Maybe it's love and maybe it isn't, but time will certainly tell. And I already like what I see, so we'll just wait to see, what else happens. But you both will definitely have my support if this thing makes my grandbaby happy."

Behind them, Tierra's voice filled the warm air between them. "You two have both completely lost your minds!"

Tierra could barely focus on the road as she maneuvered her car toward downtown Dallas and her favorite shopping mall, Galleria Dallas. Travis was trying to explain the conversation Tierra had overheard between him and her grandmother. And although his arguments about the two of them becoming involved were intriguing, she was having no part of it.

"Why not?" Travis queried, turning in his seat to stare at her.

"I can't believe you'd ask me that. Pray tell, what part of your plan makes an ounce of sense?"

"All of it. We start by dating, and after a respectable amount of time I'll ask you to marry me. You'll say yes. We'll have a beautiful wedding and eventually three kids and a dog. It makes perfect sense to me."

"Marry you! I know you're crazy now!" Tierra shook her head.

Travis grinned broadly. The idea hadn't seemed crazy at all when it had come to him. Marrying Tierra seemed like the most sensible thing he could do. He certainly wasn't going to risk losing her. Making her his wife, the two of them tied to each other for eternity, was not only logical but fantastical, as well. When he considered the circumstances of how they'd become acquainted and their growing friendship, marriage was the least crazy thing he could imagine.

"No, Tierra, I'm very serious. I want you to be my wife," he said, self-satisfaction holding hands with his words.

"What part of me getting dumped at the altar didn't you get? It was just a few short days ago that I was engaged to marry another man. A man I loved very much."

"You might have cared about him, but you weren't in love with him."

Tierra bristled. "I'm not in love with you."

Travis smiled. "Are you sure about that? Because I think you might be, and your granny agrees with me. Admit it. It was love at first sight, girl!"

"And that's another thing," Tierra stated as she pulled into a city parking lot, found an empty space and slammed hard on the brakes. "Where do you get off drawing my grandmother into your craziness?"

Tierra shifted the car into Park and shut off the engine. Turning to face the man, she crossed her arms over her chest and waited for a response.

Travis laughed. "Mama Dee asked me a question and I answered it. I don't know why you're having such a problem, Tierra."

Exasperated, Tierra threw her arms up in frustration. "Aargh!" she shouted, her eyes widening as she stared at him. Shaking her head, she pushed her way out of the car and slammed the door.

Travis was growing used to the woman's tantrums. Exiting the vehicle, he raced behind her to catch up. As he reached her side he swept her hand into his and held it.

Shaking him off, Tierra gave him an evil stare. Travis laughed.

"You really aren't funny," Tierra said.

"I have my moments. So, where are we headed now?"

Cutting her eyes at him, Tierra scowled, the frown clouding her face. "I have to return the wedding bands I purchased. Is that going to be a problem?"

Travis grinned. "Not at all. In fact, while we're here we can pick out a new pair. We might need them sooner than later."

Reaching for her hand a second time, Travis clasped her fingers gently between his own. Tierra's first instinct was to pull away again but she didn't. Whether she admitted it out loud or not, she liked holding Travis's hand, even if the man was annoying.

Travis followed Tierra faithfully as she moved from one store in the large shopping complex to another. Their first stop had been Bachendorf's Jewelers. With its extensive collection of handcrafted designer jewelry, Travis could easily see what had drawn Tierra to the nicely detailed gold bands that she'd selected. The 18-karat gold had been nice. The diamonds and platinum he planned to put on her hand would be much nicer, he thought, making a mental note to come back for a matching set that had caught his eye.

Tierra balked when Travis insisted she try on the engagement ring and wedding band set.

"Just to see," Travis said, refusing to let her waffle her way out of it. "I like them and I just want to see them on a woman's hand."

"Well, you need to go find you another woman to experiment with," Tierra said, trying to move down toward the other end of the counter.

As Travis clasped her by the elbow, she knew there would be no backing down without causing a major scene. The man had her once again, and the expression that crossed her face said she wasn't happy about it.

"Your boyfriend is very persistent," the redheaded sales clerk said with a slight chuckle. "And he has impeccable taste. This set is an interlocking engagement ring and wedding band combination. It's solid platinum with a 6.78 carat, princess-cut diamond and twenty-four diamond baguettes. It's a stunning piece of jewelry and looks wonderful on."

"He's not my boyfriend," Tierra muttered as she cut her eye at Travis.

The woman raised her eyebrows curiously as Travis nodded his head in contradiction.

Suddenly intrigued, Tierra slowly extended her left hand in the woman's direction. Shaking her head, she wanted to tell Travis exactly what she thought about him, but it would have to wait until they were back in the car, and alone. Right then she needed to try on a ring to appease him.

From the jewelry store they'd gone on to a gift shop, a Hallmark greeting cards store, Ann Taylor, Old Navy and Cache. Travis couldn't believe how much stuff Tierra had needed to return.

"Are you keeping anything?" he finally asked as they maneuvered their way in the direction of Saks Fifth Avenue.

"What do you mean?"

"Anything you purchased. Are you keeping anything, or is this like some pity-party ritual you women do? Buy to make the hurt go away and then burn back to the store before the credit card bill is due."

Tierra rolled her eyes. "Don't start."

"I was just asking."

"Well, don't. And I am not having a pity party. There is just no reason to hold on to things that I have no use for. Why waste money?"

"You knew you had no use for some of that junk when you were buying it. But you bought it anyway."

"Tch!" Tierra sucked her teeth, her face skewed with displeasure. She hastened her steps, wanting to leave Travis somewhere behind.

"So, where are we headed to now?" he asked, racing to catch up to her.

"This is my last stop," she said, entering the lingerie department of Saks Fifth Avenue. "Then I'm taking you back to the ranch, and this is going to be the last time you ride shotgun with me."

Travis shrugged, a broad grin pulling at his lips. "If you say so," he said, his grin widening further as he looked around. "I'll just be over here," he said, moving in the opposite direction. Tierra headed to the sales counter with the last of her returns, a sexy negligee that would have been a part of her honeymoon trousseau.

Minutes later as she stood waiting for the salesclerk to refund her credit card, Travis moved to her side with a La Perla push-up bra and matching thong.

"Now, this would be hot on you!" he exclaimed excitedly.

Eyeing the delicate lace and dotted stretch tulle garment, Tierra didn't know whether to blush or drop down into a hole in the floor from embarrassment. She couldn't believe the man's gall.

"Have you completely lost your mind?" Tierra hissed, reaching for the garment that Travis was waving about so brazenly.

Travis beamed, his eyes narrowing with devilment, as he snatched it out of her reach. "Seeing you in this might make me lose my mind."

"You are never going to see me in that, Travis. Never." Tierra turned her back to the man, strumming her fingers impatiently against the counter.

"It's a size 34-A. It looked like it would be the right size for you," he teased, twirling the garment's hanger in midair. "But you can try it on if you want."

Tierra was ready to scream, and just as she was about to say so, the salesclerk returned with her credit slip in hand.

"We're sorry that didn't work out for you, Ms. Braddy. Is there anything else we can assist you with today?"

"Yes," Travis interjected. "I would like to buy this set," he said, pushing the bra and thong in the woman's direction. "And is black the only color it comes in?"

"This particular style is only in black, sir, but we have a similar set by Chantelle that comes in a wonderful shade of red."

Travis nodded excitedly. “Now that’s what I’m talkin’ ’bout!” Travis exclaimed. “We’ll take a set of those, as well. A size 34-A, please.”

“I’ll ring those right up for you, sir!”

Travis winked at the woman as he tossed his own credit card down on the counter.

As the woman walked away, Tierra leaned forward to whisper in Travis’s ear. “Looks like you’re the one who’s going to have to return junk he didn’t need to buy,” she hissed.

She moved toward the store’s entrance. “And, for the record, I take a B-cup!” she whispered loudly, tossing him a heated look over her shoulder.

Chapter 9

Tierra was still seething as she sat in the car waiting for Travis to return. When the man finally appeared, that stupid grin still plastered on his face, it took everything she had to contain herself.

Travis opened the car's rear passenger door, depositing his Saks Fifth Avenue bag onto the seat. As Tierra started the engine, she was tempted to hit the gas and leave him standing there looking stupid. As he slid into the seat beside her, still smiling widely, she snarled.

"You absolutely infuriate me," she said, cutting her eye at him as she pulled out of the parking spot.

"That's because you like me," Travis said nonchalantly. "You remember what it was like in grade school when a boy had a crush on you and he'd give you a hard time or you'd give the boy a hard time? You two liked each other but you didn't want to show it."

"You don't have a clue what you're talking about," Tierra said as she gunned the engine down the highway.

"I know more than you think," Travis said casually.

Silence filled the space between them. Just as Tierra motioned to turn on the radio to take some of the awkward quiet away, Travis stopped her, his hand tapping gently against the back of hers.

"Tell me about you and Damien," he said, turning in his seat to stare at her.

"I really don't want to talk about him."

"Do it anyway. It's important."

"Why?"

"Do you have to argue every point, Tierra? I just want to know about your relationship with Private Porter."

Cutting her eye at him again, Tierra saw that he was studying her intently, a look of seriousness blanketing his expression.

She sighed, filling her lungs with air. "I was twelve when we first met," Tierra started. "He lived next door to my grandmother and he and my brother became best friends."

"When did you two start dating?"

"A little in high school and then in college it got serious." Tierra paused, her thoughts suddenly racing. Beside her, Travis cleared his throat, motioning for her to continue.

"When things were good between us, they were very good. Damien was the epitome of romantic. He always said the right thing. He showered me with affection. He made me laugh. Do you know he'd recite poetry to me, and once I came home to find four dozen red roses scattered around my house. He was also good at surprising me with little trinkets when I least expected them. I thought he was my friend and I trusted him. It was everything a girl could have wanted from a guy." Tierra blew a gust of warm breath past her lips.

Travis nodded his head. "Why do you think it didn't work?"

Tierra shrugged, her wistful tone shifting into indifference. "Damien has issues with fidelity. He thinks cheating should be a professional sport."

"You deserve better than that."

"I know," Tierra said with a deep sigh. "I just didn't want to admit to myself that he was such a jerk. I allowed myself to get caught up in the fantasy of what I wanted our relationship to be. I was hoping he would change. I wanted to believe that he loved me enough to do better."

"I think you knew that wasn't going to happen," Travis said, eyeing her closely. "Didn't you?"

Tierra met his gaze. With no need to answer his question, she changed the subject. "What about you? There's no woman in your life?"

Travis shook his head. "Nope. I've never really had time for a relationship. I've dated, but no one serious. The military has been my one and only mistress."

"No one? Not even before the military?"

"Not a soul, unless you count Paula Liston from high school. I took Paula to the prom."

"And where is Paula Liston now?"

"Married with four kids and living in Danbury, Connecticut, the last I heard."

"Your mother hasn't pressured you to get married and have kids?"

"My mother died a few years ago. Breast cancer. My dad passed away when I was a little kid. That's why I spent so much time with my cousins and my uncle, before he and his wife were killed in a car wreck."

"I'm so sorry," Tierra said, a wave of sadness washing over her. "Tingin and I lost our parents young, as well. Our father disappeared shortly after we were born. Never knew much of anything about him. Our mother sent us to live with Mama Dee when it became too much for her to handle."

"Is she still alive? Your mother?"

Tierra shrugged. "We don't know. We lost touch with her many, many years ago. Mama Dee became the only mother we ever knew."

Travis nodded. "Your grandmother is a special lady."

Tierra nodded her agreement. "You and your cousins seem to be very close."

Grinning broadly, Travis nodded. "We are. They're more like brothers than cousins. In fact, I'm hoping they'll all stand up for us at our wedding."

"Do you ever give up?" Tierra questioned, a light giggle passing over her lips. "You are absolutely ridiculous."

"If I don't marry you, Tierra Braddy, I'll never get you into that lingerie I bought, and that stuff was expensive! Did you know how expensive that was? That purchase was basically equivalent to a month's pay!"

Tierra laughed. "You are so crazy! I told you not to buy that stuff."

Travis laughed with her. "You know you wanted it. 'I take a B-cup!'" he said, mimicking her.

"I did not!" Tierra gushed, laughter building between them.

"Oh, yes you did!"

The rest of the ride back to the ranch was pleasant as the two exchanged stories, allowing themselves to relax in each other's company. As Tierra pulled her car into the driveway, Travis marveled at the level of comfort they could easily find with each other. But knowing Tierra, he also knew that it would only last so long before she'd be fighting him, and her feelings, again.

The wedding chapel was a charming structure built back in the late 1920s. The remodel, which included replacing all the original clapboard siding was just days from being complete, and as Tierra stepped through the double wooden doors she couldn't help but be impressed by the beauty of the interior.

The cedar pews had been polished to a high shine, the coloration a rich red mahogany. Newly installed stained-glass windows shimmered color across the walls. A runner of red carpet atop the hardwood floors ran the length of the center aisle. It would have made a perfect venue for a wedding.

Allowing herself to slip into the fantasy, Tierra imagined the moment she would have walked down the aisle. In her mind's eye she saw herself dressed in her beautiful gown, her hair and makeup meticulous. She would be wearing her grandmother's pearls, the double strand that rested in the matriarch's treasured jewelry box. Those pearls would be the something old she'd need for good luck.

Her something blue, the color of a robin's egg, would be hidden beneath her gown, awaiting her new husband's eyes when she slipped out of her dress after the reception. She hadn't yet figured out her something borrowed or the something new.

Tierra dreamt of the moment when she would ease forward toward her groom, the man she would promise her unconditional love. Just weeks before, she had known who he would be. Now she wasn't sure what she knew.

Easing her way slowly down the carpeted aisle, Tierra brushed her fingers across the top of each bench until she reached the first one, which sat mere inches from the altar. Thinking about the wedding day she'd planned for herself, Tierra fantasized the floral arrangements, the musical selections and the friends and family who would have been there to celebrate in her joy.

Stepping before the altar, Tierra closed her eyes. Her breathing was slow and even as she recited her wedding vows over and over again in her head. She would have promised her soul mate her heart and soul, pledging to be a loving and adoring wife. Her wedding would have been perfect. Now she couldn't imagine her groom.

That man calling her name interrupted her thoughts. When she opened her eyes, Travis stood at her side studying her intently.

Tierra's gaze met his and held it, falling fast into the adoration that gleamed down on her. His cool stare was caressing, washing an easy energy through her soul. She could have stayed lost in the deep stare he was giving her.

He posed his question to her a second time. "How are you holding up?"

"I'm hanging in here."

The man nodded as he lifted his eyes to stare around the room. "It's quite spectacular," he said, taking in the view.

Tierra smiled her assent.

Travis continued. "You made a great choice."

"I don't recall asking for your opinion."

The look he gave her was teasing. "I would think you'd want your future husband's opinion. Most especially about where we would be getting married."

Tierra rolled her eyes skyward, turning an about-face to stare toward the windows. She was determined not to coddle his delusions.

"I really wish you would stop following me," she said, refusing to meet his gaze.

Stepping in behind her, Travis pressed his hands to her shoulders. His touch was strong, engaging Tierra's senses despite her desire to ignore him. Unable to resist, Tierra leaned back against his chest as Travis wrapped his arms around her, drawing her closely to him. In that very moment she was suddenly desperate to be held.

When the man pressed a kiss to the back of her neck, Tierra was totally gone. Never before had she felt so much love washing over her. Turning to face him, she leaned her head into his chest as Travis squeezed her tighter. The two stood in the embrace for some time, each holding tight to the other as if their lives depended on it.

As time came to a complete standstill, Tierra found

herself staring once again into the man's eyes, cradled by the deep stare he was giving her. For the first time in a long time, Tierra felt like she'd found her way home where she was most safe and secure.

Moving as if to kiss her mouth, Travis hesitated, his head leaning in close and pulling back. With her excitement mounting, Tierra's lips parted ever so slightly. The second time he leaned in, Travis pressed his mouth to hers, kissing her easily. Tierra found herself lost in the moment, the sweet caress sweeter than sweet nectar.

The man tasted like icy mint, and as his lips skated across her own, she couldn't remember what it was like to kiss anyone else, nor could she imagine herself ever kissing another man again. The emotion both surprised and confused her.

With his mouth dancing a soft tango, Travis traced the outline of her mouth with his tongue, probing gently as he parted her lips. A rift of pleasure shot through his bloodstream when Tierra opened her mouth to him, her own tongue eagerly dancing with his.

The moment was surreal as the two stood before the church altar, sunlight shimmering warmth over the two of them. When Travis tightened his arms around her, his large hands caressing her back, Tierra's good sense kicked into high gear with a vengeance. She pressed her small palms against the expanse of his chest and pushed him from her. As the connection between them broke, Travis opened his eyes. Both were breathing heavily, panting for a hint of air to cool the sudden rise of heat that felt like it wanted to consume them.

Travis cupped his hand against her face, his fingers caressing the line of her profile. Moving as if to kiss her again, Travis was suddenly surprised when Tierra shook her head vehemently, turned around abruptly and bolted from the room.

"Tierra! Tierra!" He called her name again and again but she ignored him. For a quick minute Travis thought about chasing behind her, and then he changed his mind. He imagined it would take Tierra some time to process what had just happened between them.

Dropping down against an empty pew, Travis took a deep breath, filling his lungs with warm air as he sat in reflection. Kissing Tierra had been a dream come true. Kissing her there, in that space, would be even sweeter the day she became his wife.

With her fingers pressed against her lips, Tierra couldn't believe she'd allowed that man to kiss her. Nor could she believe how much she had enjoyed it. As she raced down the bricked walkway to the passage of yard and grass that bordered the property's home, she couldn't shake the sensation of Travis's hands and mouth burning hot against her skin. Her stomach was still doing flips, rolling with pleasure from having been touched.

Just as she reached the home's patio, she came to a standstill. She shook her arms down to her sides, trying to shake the anxiety from her system. She didn't want to have to explain anything to Eden or her sisters. She wasn't much interested in anyone knowing what had just happened between her and Travis.

She blew a deep sigh, moving to one of the cushioned lounge chairs that adorned the rear patio. Her knees were still quivering from the excitement of having such an incredible man show that kind of interest in her. But there had to be something completely wrong with her being interested in Travis Stallion. It just had to be her rebounding from her failed relationship with what's-his-name. She couldn't begin to believe it was anything more.

Chapter 10

Tierra climbed up to sit atop the railing of the wooden fence that surrounded the blue-green pasture. The horses were grazing, chewing at the soft grass that decorated the landscape. The evening air was slowly starting to cool from the day's heat, a cool breeze blowing in a soft gust.

Lost in thought, she was startled for a brief moment thinking she heard the wind calling out her name, and then she realized it was Travis calling. The man was moving in her direction, his gait slow and easy with just a hint of a dip in his step. Tierra like the way he moved, his stride as graceful as a dancer's but with a mountain of masculine bravado and a seductive rhythm that spoke volumes about his confidence level. He was sexy as hell, and watching him move one instinctively knew that he was a man who knew how to use his body.

As he came up beside her, his hand pressing hot against her knee, Tierra thought she might combust from the swell of heat that had suddenly consumed her. She couldn't remember the last time any man had her so hot that moisture was puddling in places she didn't know moisture could reach. His touch was almost too much for her to handle as she shifted her body from his, lifting her leg from beneath his touch.

"I'm sorry," Travis said softly, his gaze meeting hers. "I didn't mean to upset you, Tierra."

She took a deep breath of warm air. "I'm not upset. I would really just like to be left alone, Travis."

Her eyes skated back and forth across the fields, fighting to stare at anything except Travis.

Bemused, the man touched her a second time, his fingers softly kneading her flesh. The unconscious gesture only served to infuriate her more.

"Why do you keep doing that?" Tierra exclaimed, jumping down from the fence and squaring off against him.

"What?"

"Why do you keep touching me? Do you always go around putting your hands on people?"

Travis smiled, the bend of his mouth so sweet that Tierra was suddenly hungry for a little taste of the man's honey and sugar. Her eyes widened, a wave of something she'd never felt before washing over her spirit. The intensity of it was startling.

"Aargh!" Tierra screamed as she spun away from him, almost racing in the other direction. "I can't stand you!"

Behind her, Travis stood with his arms crossed over his chest, shaking his head. He absolutely adored her spirited energy.

Travis stood beneath a spray of hot water, the heated moisture washing over his head, rolling down his broad back and chest to trickle in small puddles at his feet. After an exceptionally long day, the water felt good. He could have stood there for the rest of the evening, but it was boy's night out and he was anxious to get some male perspective on his present situation with Tierra.

He was certain his cousins would call him crazy. If he were honest with himself he was only feeling but so rational at the moment. Marriage. It had seemed like a great idea when it first came to his mind, and it still did. The thought of him and Tierra spending the rest of their lives together intrigued him. What he found himself feeling for the woman was even more captivating. The fact that it had all happened so quickly was completely mystifying. He was experiencing a rash of emotions like he'd never experienced before, and despite the absurdity of it all, every ounce of it felt like the most natural thing in the world.

Mrs. Travis Stallion. He'd always had a vivid image of the woman who he would love so hard that he would want her to carry his name. His mother had been a shining example of what he wanted for himself in a partner and companion. A young Abigail Tatum had given his father, Joseph Stallion, a real run for the man's money before she'd given in to his charm, agreeing to be his wife.

But Abigail and Joseph hadn't had a whirlwind

romance. Abigail had told Travis often how his father had dragged his feet for years before realizing that Abigail was the woman of his dreams. It had only been when she'd given up on the two of them completely, testing the waters by dating other men, that Joseph had seen the errors of his way. That's when Abigail had dug in her heels, making the man jump through hoops to regain her affections.

Travis had always marveled at how much they'd known about each other, often finishing the other's thoughts and reading each other's minds. The couple had loved each other deeply. Travis had grown up knowing that one day he would want that for himself with a woman who duplicated his mother's fiery spirit and no-nonsense demeanor. Tierra embodied many of his mother's attributes and more.

Tierra excited him and he was curious to see what the future had in store for them as each other's partner, best friend, companion and lover. No matter what it took, he was convinced that Tierra Braddy was destined to be the future Mrs. Travis Stallion.

Travis drew his hands over his body, lathering his skin with an almond-scented body wash. He tilted his face into the spray of warm water, the fluid rinsing suds over his broad shoulders and down the length of his back. He suddenly imagined himself standing beneath a spray of water with Tierra, the woman's naked body pressed against his own, kissing her like he'd kissed her earlier that day. He wished it were her flesh beneath his fingers, his touch lingering against the softness of her skin. Fantasizing had hardened every one of his muscles, the wanting causing his blood to boil hot through his veins.

Reaching for the faucet, Travis turned the water from hot to cold, cringing as the chilling fluid hit him. If nothing else, he thought, allowing the cold to wash thoughts of Tierra and that kiss from his mind, he had to do something about that woman soon.

Tierra stood staring out at the view of the city from her apartment window. She hadn't planned on returning home as soon as she had, but she needed extra clothes for her short sabbatical at the Stallion family ranch. She had also needed to hang her wedding gown in the closet, having finally found the resolve to retrieve it from the bridal shop. A late-night dinner with his cousin Matthew had been the only thing to keep Travis from following behind her. The man had been like a thorn in her side since he'd declared himself her chief protector and personal bodyguard.

As she stood there, dressed in her Monique Lhuillier wedding gown, she couldn't help but note that it had been well over a week since the man had walked into her life, and ever since that first day everything in her existence had changed. Even more important, none of it was making any sense to her.

She moved back to the full-length mirror to stare at her reflection. The strapless, one-piece, full A-line gown with its corset closure and ruched bodice featured a sweetheart neckline and dropped waist trimmed with embellished lace motifs. The skirt boasted three voluptuous gathered tiers of organza. It was the most beautiful thing she had ever worn, and Tierra had known the moment she first tried it on that it was meant for her to wear on her wedding day. She blew a soft sigh, thoughts of Travis suddenly wafting through her head again.

Travis was still rationalizing reasons the two of them should think about marriage. The man was almost convincing, but Tierra continued to brush his insistence off, choosing to believe that the man was simply poking fun at her.

Tierra had to admit, though, that the notion made her smile. And it didn't help that her grandmother had taken a shine to Travis, treating him as if he were the next best thing since the baking of white bread.

The matriarch had called her just minutes before to reiterate the virtues of Travis Stallion. Tierra shook her head as she thought back to the conversation.

"Did you see Travis today?" her granny had asked curiously. "He's such a sweet young man!" she'd exclaimed for the umpteenth time.

"He's really not that sweet, Mama Dee."

"He's got a nice disposition, plus he's skilled and educated, and he has impeccable manners. He's definitely got more going for him than that other one ever did."

"Please, don't start, Mama Dee."

"I'm just saying."

"Is that why you called me, just to say?"

"Don't be a wiseass, Tierra. You ain't that grown."

Tierra heaved a deep sigh. "Yes, ma'am. I apologize."

"Maybe Travis would like to come for dinner

this week. I do expect you and Tingin to join me on Wednesday."

"I don't know, Mama Dee. I'll have to get back to you about that."

"He's a good man, Tierra."

"Yes, ma'am, I'm sure he is, but it's not like that between us."

"You won't know what it's like if you don't allow yourself to be open to the possibilities."

"But, Mama—"

"But nothing. Think about it, Tierra, and when you're done thinking about it, then pray on it. Pray long and hard and you'll know exactly what to do."

Tierra had nodded her head into the telephone receiver. "Yes, ma'am."

Mama Dee had continued. "I honestly believe the man loves you, Tierra. And I believe you've fallen in love with him, too."

Tierra had shaken her head, making a mental note to call her brother to ask if he thought they might need to have their family physician give the old woman a psychiatric evaluation. Her grandmother was clearly as crazy as a loon. And the fact that Tierra had actually given the idea of her and Travis being in a relationship together some consideration wasn't saying much for her sanity, either.

Tierra giggled softly at the thought, her head still shaking. Taking a deep breath, she slid out of her wedding gown, placing it carefully back into its zippered bag. As she hung it in her guest room closet, her hand lingered against it for a brief moment, one solitary tear drop rolling over the round of her cheek.

Chapter 11

Breakfast in bed had become a ritual for the couple. Since that first morning, Travis had awakened her each morning with a plate of something decadent in his hands as he stood in the entrance to her room. This morning was no exception, as he knocked on the door and then burst inside without waiting for a response, the sweet aroma of blueberry muffins teasing the early day air.

Tierra was better prepared, though, fully clothed in a pair of flannel sleeping pants and a tank top as she sat upright in one of the cushioned wingback chairs awaiting his arrival. She couldn't help but smile back as the man greeted her with a charmed grin.

"Good morning, beautiful."

"Sergeant Stallion, good morning to you."

"Did you sleep well?"

Tierra nodded. "Exceptionally well. How about yourself?"

He shrugged, the thought crossing his mind that he would have slept much better had she been curled up against his body. He bit back the desire to say so. "So, what's on our agenda today?"

As Tierra took a bite of her muffin, following it with a sip of freshly squeezed orange juice, she shook her head. After swallowing the mouthful of food, she answered. "Not a thing. I plan to wash my hair and just sit back and relax. If I do anything, I may go horseback riding, but that will probably be it."

Travis dropped down on to the bed, crossing his leg over his knee as he stared at her. "We can do that."

"There's no *we* in this, Travis. That's what *I* am doing," Tierra said, emphasizing her desire to not include him in her plans. "I don't know what *you* are doing."

Travis laughed. "I am washing your hair."

A bite of muffin caught in Tierra's throat, choking her momentarily. She coughed into her inner elbow.

"You okay?" Travis questioned, leaning toward her.

Tierra nodded. "I'm fine. Why must everything be a joint effort with you? You're driving me crazy!"

"We don't have much time left before I deploy again, Tierra. I'm trying to take advantage of every moment."

The woman heaved a deep sigh. "Well, I'm going to wash my hair in the shower, and I can do that all by myself. But thank you for offering."

"Even better," Travis exclaimed, rising to his feet. "Let's get started," he said excitedly.

Tierra shook her head vehemently. "I don't know what you have in mind, Travis, but the answer is no!"

The man ignored her, chuckling to himself as he

headed into her bathroom. Tierra could hear him turning on the water, adjusting the flow of hot and cold. He called out her name. "Let's go, Tierra!"

She couldn't begin to fathom what the man had to be thinking. Breakfast was one thing, but this was something else all together. "You're crazy," she admonished. "I really can take a shower all by myself."

"And I can take one with you while I wash your hair," the man responded matter-of-factly.

Tierra's eyes widened in astonishment as Travis suddenly stripped out of his jeans and dropped them to the floor. Pulling his T-shirt over his head, he stood in nothing but a snow-white pair of boxer briefs.

The man was clearly a work of art. The lines of his torso were picture-perfect, his sculpted form breathtakingly beautiful. There was a faint scar that ran a few short inches down his abdomen, but that was the only blemish that appeared to mar his complexion. The defining bulge of his manhood drew her attention, the apex heralding his thick thighs and toned calves.

"I can get completely naked if you'd like," Travis said casually, his thumbs tucked into the waistband of his briefs. "Or not, depending on what you'd prefer."

The butterflies in Tierra's stomach suddenly turned into a flock of birds. "I really don't know about this," Tierra said, her calm, easy tone contradicting the strained expression on her face. "This is absurd, Travis Stallion!"

"So, it's not conventional, but the last few days have been quite unconventional, as well. But hey, what do you have to lose? It'll be an experience we can tell our grandchildren about someday."

"We're not having grandchildren."

Travis smiled, the sweet gesture washing warmth over her. "At least not for a few years. Now, are you going to get in the shower or not? You can keep all your clothes on if you want, although it will probably be easier if you at least stripped down to your undies."

Travis couldn't take his eyes off Tierra. She was staring at him as if he were crazy, and for a brief moment he would have thought so himself. He didn't know what he'd been thinking until the words had come out of his mouth. And now, standing half-naked hoping that she might join him had him completely questioning his own best judgment. With nothing to lose, he winked at her and gestured for her to step into the shower.

This is crazy, Tierra thought, the words spinning through her head over and over again. But her body suddenly moved of its own accord, disregarding the voice in the back of her head that told her to run and run fast. With a mind of their own, her fingers reached for the belt at her waist and loosened the tie on her sleeping pants, allowing the flannel slacks to fall to the floor at her feet. In only her bikini briefs and her tank top, she slowly moved in Travis's direction. Her delicate steps were alluring, teasing every one of the man's senses.

As she stared into his eyes, Travis's desire was plain to see, although Tierra was too consumed with her own wanting to rationalize what he might have been feeling. Watching as the man had stripped out of his clothes had given her a rush like she'd never experienced before. Beneath the tank top she was wearing her nipples had hardened and stuck out like little soldiers. Tierra resisted the urge to press her palms to her breasts, not wanting to draw attention to her own predicament. Easing past him, she stepped into the shower and Travis stepped in behind her.

Standing side by side in the glassed enclosure, the two stood staring at each other, neither knowing what to do next. The moment wasn't what either had expected. Travis suddenly felt foolish, and Tierra couldn't believe she'd actually gone along with him. She suddenly burst out laughing, the hilarity of the moment consuming her. Ripples of mirth started deep in her midsection and swelled full and thick between them. Enthralled, Travis couldn't help but join her, and within minutes the two were laughing hysterically until tears began to flow from both their eyes.

"So, what next?" Travis managed to ask, gasping for a deep breath of air.

The young woman shrugged. "Since we're here," she said, the amusement still painting her expression, "you might as well wash my hair."

Tierra ducked her head under the warm spray and the soothing water saturated her hair in seconds. Reaching for the bottle of shampoo, she turned to face him. She extended the container in his direction, and when he pulled it from her hands she took one step closer. When their bodies touched, neither thought to draw away.

Moving against her, Travis filled the palm of his hand with the shea butter shampoo and gently rubbed it through the shoulder-length strands. As he slowly massaged her scalp with his fingers, the thick lather ran in rivulets down her caramel body.

Closing her eyes, Tierra leaned into the tenderness of his strokes. Travis was massaging her head gently, and each time his fingers parted the silken strands and lightly caressed her scalp, the sweetness of his touch caused her spirit to soar and swell with sheer delight. The skill with which he washed and rinsed her hair and the erotic bravado of his body just millimeters from her own caused her to quiver with wanting like she'd never known before. It also didn't help that Travis was suddenly sporting a rock-hard erection that seemed to be straining for her full and undivided attention.

Opening her eyes, Tierra met his deep gaze. His expression was pained as he struggled to regain a semblance of control over his own body. Sensing his obvious discomfort, Tierra couldn't help but smile, a smug grin that made Travis raise his eyebrows.

"What?"

Tierra couldn't stall the giggle that bubbled past her lips. "Looks like you've got a personal problem to deal with."

Her eyes dropped to his crotch for a brief second before rising back to his face. A rash of red color flushed the man's cheeks.

"You seem to have one of your own," he whispered as he stared directly at her chest, her breasts clearly visible through her wet top. Without giving it a thought, Travis cupped his palm around the soft tissue, allowing his thumb to graze the rock-candy delight that protruded so blatantly. The heat from his hands burned hot against her flesh, flooding her whole body with ardor. Tierra inhaled swiftly, his touch surprising and enthralling her at the same time.

"What are you—?" Tierra started, as Travis moved from one nipple to the other, leaning to press his lips against the inner curve of her right breast. Her eyes widened at the sensations that suddenly swept through every nerve ending. She suddenly felt light-headed, her knees threatening to drop her where she stood. She heard someone in the room moan and then realized the soft whimper had slipped past her own lips.

Scarcely breathing, and ever so gently, Travis moved an arm over and across her body to pull her closer. He eased both hands around her waist, pulling her tightly against him as he wrapped her in a deep embrace. Emboldened, he nuzzled his cheek against her cheek, then gently kissed her forehead as his hands danced across her shoulders and down the length of her arms. Consumed by the moment, Tierra wrapped her small hands around his thick torso, her fingers gently caressing his bare back. The taut muscles seemed to pulse against her fingertips as she hugged him back.

Confusion suddenly washed over her senses. Sexual tension had risen like an enormous beast between them, needing to be fed and nourished lest it explode with a vengeance. Whatever was happening shouldn't have been. He had no business toying with her so wantonly. She had no business reveling in his touch so unabashedly. Neither one of them had any business being in such a compromising position.

Travis felt her tense in his arms. Sensing her change of heart, he leaned to whisper into her ear.

"What's the matter, Tierra?" he asked, his lips grazing the lobe of her ear.

Tierra's head shook vehemently from side to side. "We shouldn't be doing this," she hissed softly.

Travis sighed. Taking a step back, he stared down

at her. He cupped his hands around her cheeks, tilting her gaze up to his. "I want you, Tierra, and I know you want me. I can feel it."

Tierra couldn't stop herself from shaking, her body quivering as if she were cold. She crossed her arms over her chest, wrapping them around her torso. "I can't do this," she answered. "It's not…it's…it's just not right, Travis."

"Tierra, you're wrong. You know this is right," he repeated, his tone adamant. "You know it and feel it just like I do."

"I don't know anything of the sort." This time she stepped backward until her back was pressed against the glass.

"Do you want me to stop, Tierra?"

"We shouldn't be doing this," she repeated.

Travis moved toward her, his hand reaching out to caress her cheek. "Tierra, I love you."

Her voice rose shrilly as she pulled away from his touch. "I said no, Travis!"

Travis's gaze swept over her face. Water sprayed over them from the large showerhead in the wall, catching Tierra's tears as they flowed into the drain. Nodding his head slowly, Travis backed his way out of the shower.

Turning an about-face, he reached for a plush towel that rested on the countertop and wrapped it around his waist. Bending to retrieve his clothes, he tossed her one last look, and before Tierra could think to change her mind, Travis Stallion disappeared out of the room.

Chapter 12

It had been three whole days since the incident in the shower and Tierra still hadn't seen Travis. Each morning she'd sat waiting for him to deliver breakfast, and not long after it was time for lunch she would give up hope that he might actually appear. Even his family was beginning to question where the man might have disappeared to.

"John, what's up with Travis?" Marah asked as she took a seat at the family dining table. She took a sip of her sweetened tea.

Hearing the man's name, Tierra looked up from her chicken salad and fresh fruit, her stare focused on John's face as she waited anxiously for him to answer.

Still staring at the newspaper he was reading, John shrugged animatedly as he answered, "He headed down to the lake to do some fly-fishing. Something about needing some time to himself."

Marah nodded, her eyes meeting Tierra's directly. "The last time *you* needed some time to yourself, I had to go looking for you, John Stallion." She smiled. "Tierra, the man had me flying from one coast to the other to track him down because he was pouting about absolutely nothing. Finally, when we caught up with each other, our families locked us in a limousine until we got over needing some time apart."

Tierra smiled back at the woman.

John smirked. "If you hadn't been driving me crazy in the first place, I wouldn't have had to go anyplace."

"Is that Travis's problem?" Marah asked, her gaze still focused on Tierra. "Has a woman driven him crazy?"

Lowering the newspaper into his lap, John looked from one woman to the other. Tierra's face was red, a wave of embarrassment washing over her. The man shook his head. "I think that whatever is bothering Travis will work itself out when it needs to." The man locked eyes with his wife as he directed his comments at Tierra.

"Tierra, please do not let my wife talk you into anything foolish. Marah thinks playing matchmaker means interfering in other people's business. I'm sure you and Travis will work things out when you're both ready." He winked an all-knowing eye at her.

"It's not like that," Tierra exclaimed. "I mean..." She paused. She honestly didn't know what she meant. She only knew that she was missing Travis. She was missing him very much. She blew a deep sigh, pushing her plate away.

Marah was still staring at her. "Well, it's definitely a

pretty day to spend out on the lake. Did Travis say when he was coming back?"

John rose from his seat, folding his newspaper neatly before resting it against the tabletop. "Stay out of it, Marah!"

As he moved to the door, Marah giggled. She called out her husband's name. "John Stallion!"

Turning back to face her, John grinned broadly. "He's staying in the Austin area until Monday. Something about tree houses." He turned to make his exit, and as he eased out the door he called out over his shoulder. "And you didn't hear that from me!"

When she was certain the man was out of hearing distance, Marah leaned toward Tierra, the gesture almost conspiratorial. "So, what do you plan to do, girl?"

Tierra eyed her curiously. "I don't know what you mean. What do I plan to do about what?"

"About Travis. What do you plan to do about getting your man?" As Marah answered, her sister Eden came waltzing into the room, joining in the conversation.

"Well, I'm glad someone is asking her!" Eden exclaimed.

Tierra's eyes widened. "You both have lost your minds."

Eden laughed. "Tea, it doesn't take a rocket scientist to see that something's been growing between you and Travis. You two have been tossing each other lovey-dovey eyes for days now. So what happened?"

Tierra sighed. "We...well...nothing...not really," the woman stammered, her face flooding with crimson color.

"She's fighting it," Eden said matter-of-factly, turning to her sister.

"Big-time," Marah said in concurrence. "Denial is always telling."

Eden nodded. "Sounds like the two of them need a little helping hand. What do you think, sister dear?"

"I think we need a plan," Marah answered. She looked at Tierra. "What do you think?"

Tierra's eyes skated from one friend to the other as she tossed her hands up in frustration. "I don't know what to think!"

Two hours later, Tierra was comfortably ensconced in the interior of the Stallion family jet. She still couldn't believe how quickly her friends had pulled everything together, confirming Travis's travel itinerary and coordinating Tierra's schedule to join him. The flight from Dallas to Austin would take about thirty minutes. She couldn't believe that she would be in the man's presence in less than an hour, hopefully making amends for what had happened between them. Or maybe apologizing for what she hadn't allowed to happen.

Twisting in her seat, Tierra brushed both her palms against her thighs. Travis had been right. She wanted him. She wanted him more than she had ever wanted any man. More than she had ever wanted Damien Porter. If he had pressed her, she would have willingly opened herself up to him. But he hadn't pressed. He'd walked away without as much as a backwards glance. Then he'd disappeared, leaving her alone and frustrated.

As she played everything over and over again in her head, Tierra found herself having second thoughts.

Marah and Eden's brilliant idea was starting to dull considerably. Maybe chasing after Travis Stallion wasn't such a good idea after all.

There was a cool breeze blowing over the blue-green waters of Lake Travis. The man stood thigh deep in the chilling water as it washed over the rubber waders he wore. He looped his thumbs behind the suspenders over his shoulders.

Lake Travis was one of his favorite places to be. His parents had named him after the lake, the summer vacation jaunt high on their list of places to visit. As a little boy he'd sworn the lake was his, named aptly because he possessed the rights to everything from one shore to the other. He still felt a kinship to the land and the water, both calming his spirit with little effort.

Travis took a deep inhale of air. The fresh air filled his lungs and nourished him. Thoughts of Tierra skipped through his mind. He'd been desperately trying to ignore all thoughts of her. Their last encounter had left him speechless, his frustrations exposed as he'd stood practically naked in front of her.

He couldn't begin to understand what held her back. The Tierra he'd come to know was too spirited not to act on her desires, and he'd been certain she had wanted him. For a brief moment she'd allowed herself to relax and enjoy the easy caresses that had danced against her skin. He suddenly remembered how she had pressed her pelvis against him, gyrating her body gently against his own. Heat flushed his groin at the memory.

The moment had been heated and consuming, and it had taken every ounce of fortitude he'd had not to have taken her right there in that shower stall. Then she'd said she really didn't want him. Tierra had told him no, and once told, Travis had to walk away, no longer certain about what he'd seen in her eyes.

He blew out a deep breath of exasperation. A part of him had wanted to stay, to make Tierra admit what she was feeling. Logic had moved him out of that room and as far from the woman as he could manage to go. As he'd packed his bags, sound judgment had assured him he'd made the right decision. Boarding the Stallion family jet and disembarking in Austin had given him just enough time to rationalize that he'd done the one and only thing he could possibly do.

Chasing after Tierra would have been a big mistake. Probably his biggest, and Travis was not a man who was inclined to knowingly make a mistake when such could be avoided. He'd seen too many men fall victim to their emotions, and he was not looking to be added to the statistics. The military had served him well in that respect.

He heaved another deep sigh, suddenly thinking about Jordan Burke, one of his closest friends. Jordan had been a fellow soldier whose love for his country and his service to the military had almost rivaled Travis's. The two men had graduated high school together, both enlisting in the military the moment they were able. Travis had joined the ranks of Army, his friend devoting himself to the Marines. The two had kept in touch despite their friendly rivalry, and Travis had been thrilled when Jordan had earned the rank of hospital corpsman, a position he knew his dear friend would excel in. Then a brief deployment in South America and a Brazilian beauty named Daniella had veered the man so far off course he'd been unable to find his way back.

Jordan had allowed his emotions to get in the way, and now, just a few short years later, the man was married, father to three little girls and operating a family convenience store somewhere in the Midwest. Jordan's initial dreams of retiring from the military had no longer been an option for him with the arrival of baby number one and a wife who wanted him home full-time.

Travis remembered the disappointment in his friend's voice the day the two had talked about his decision. Right then and there, Travis had sworn on everything he believed in that the military would be his first and last love, no woman ever getting in his way.

For just a brief moment he'd allowed Tierra to get under his skin. But common sense had slapped him back to reality the moment she'd rejected him. And even if he was still scratching his head at her reasons for doing so, he was willing to accept that it was for the best. It all made sense in his head, but he couldn't stall the lingering feeling in the pit of his stomach that none of it made any sense at all.

He heaved another deep sigh. Reaching for the fishing rod that rested against his leg, Travis checked the baited hook, then cast his line into the water. Fish he understood. He didn't have a clue about anything else, much less that woman.

The short balding man with the beer gut who stood waiting for her to step out of the plane smiled warmly, an amused expression blanketing his sun-kissed complexion. Tierra could tell by the smirk he was trying to hide from her that things were quickly about to go from bad to worse. She was seriously starting to rethink this impromptu trip.

"Hi," she said as casually as she could muster, trying not to draw attention to her nervousness.

"Welcome, Ms. Braddy. I'm Tucker Wells," the man said as he extended a calloused hand in her direction. "Mrs. Stallion wants me to make sure you get to your destination okay."

His deep Southern accent tickled Tierra's ears. She smiled in response.

As Tucker looked her up and down, his curious stare made her nervous. "What's wrong?" she asked, her own gaze dropping to the knee-length black skirt, white button-up blouse and black flats that she wore.

Tucker shook his head. "I'm sorry, ma'am, but did you bring something more comfortable to wear?"

"This is comfortable."

His head continued to shake. "I understand, but where you're going you might be much more comfortable in jeans and sneakers."

Nervous energy sprouted a head and tail in Tierra's abdomen, swelling through her body with a mind of its own. "Where exactly am I going? Mrs. Stallion only told me I'd be in Austin."

Tucker continued shaking his head, the unconscious tick doing nothing to ease Tierra's anxiety. "Cypress Valley, ma'am. Mr. Stallion is tree zipping."

Tierra blinked her eyes. "Tree zipping? What the heck is tree zipping?"

The man gripped her by the elbow as he led her to the jeep waiting at the end of the airstrip. “It’ll be easier, ma’am, if I just show you. But first, we need to get you changed.”

Chapter 13

Standing atop a wooden platform some forty feet high in a tree, Tierra stared out over the Texas hill country. She couldn't believe what she was about to do just to see Travis Stallion. She couldn't believe she was about to do what she was for any man.

She turned her attention from the tree-lined path to the guide who was preparing her for the next step in her adventure. "Are you sure I have to do all this to reach Mr. Stallion? I mean, can't we just call him and have him come here to us?"

The young man chuckled softly. "Sorry, ma'am. Mr. Stallion doesn't have a cell phone with him, and there are no phones in the tree houses." The teen's deep blue eyes and dimpled cheeks seemed to tease her as he smiled a deep smile.

Tierra shook her head. After she had changed into jeans and a T-shirt, Tucker had dropped her off at the

Cypress Valley Canopy Tour site, where the owners, David and Amy, had welcomed her warmly. After a few minutes of casual conversation about their love of nature and the vision that had inspired their treetop adventure, they'd placed her in the hands of their oldest son, the young man with those deep blue eyes who never stopped smiling. Now she was fitted into a harness and helmet and about to be cast off that platform on a steel-cabled zip line.

"So, tell me again, this is safe, right?" she questioned, the nervous tension rising in her voice.

"Yes, ma'am. Very safe."

"And just how high are we again?"

"We're just about forty feet off the ground."

"And how much weight do these things hold?" Tierra asked, pointing to the steel hooks she was being attached to.

"Twenty-six thousand pounds, ma'am."

Tierra could tell those blue eyes were trying not to laugh at her. She took a deep breath. "Okay…okay…I think I'm ready," she said, sucking in air as if she might be taking her last breath.

"It's going to be just fine," the man said as he gave her a gentle push.

Suddenly Tierra was zipping along a cable between the trees. She felt herself holding her breath, not sure if she wanted to scream or not. At the other end, another young guide stopped her from slamming into the tree, greeting her with a "good job" as she came to rest atop the next platform.

The boy with the blue eyes zipped in behind her,

landing easily at her side. "See," he said teasingly. "Told you it was a piece of cake!"

Tierra laughed. "Okay, so now where are we going?" she queried.

The guide pointed off into the distance. "You have to traverse six more zip lines and three sky bridges to get to Lofthaven. That's where Mr. Stallion is staying. It's our tree-house bed-and-breakfast."

"In a tree?"

"Yes, ma'am."

Tierra heaved a deep sigh. She couldn't begin to fathom what she had gotten herself into.

Travis heard her scream before he saw her. His cousin John had sent a message through the front office that Tierra was coming. For a brief moment he'd actually considered packing up his things and leaving, but he had to admit he wanted to see her. He wanted to see her bad. He was also amused that she would go to such an extreme to see him. Although it was a lot of fun, zipping wasn't for everyone.

Peering out through the open air structure, he waved his hand at the guide who had just sent Tierra in his direction. That last glide onto the tree-house platform was close to three hundred feet in length. Tierra was still screaming when he reached out to pull her atop the landing. Her eyes were wide, exhilaration pumping energy through her bloodstream.

"I used to be afraid of heights," Tierra said, meeting his gaze, her body pressed against his as he made sure she'd gotten her footing.

"And you're not anymore," Travis answered softly.

She shook her head. "No."

The two stood quietly together, neither moving. Around them the afternoon sun glistened through the leafy canopy of trees, light filtering over the land in streams. A bird chirped loudly from one of the tree limbs and water rippled over the rocks in the creek ravine below.

"Hi," Tierra said finally.

"Hi."

"So, are you surprised to see me?" Tierra asked, trying to fight the nervousness that was threatening to swallow her whole.

Travis shook his head. "No."

"They told you I was coming?"

He nodded. "Yes."

Tierra didn't say anything else, her stare never wavering. Travis smiled.

"I'm glad you did," he said finally. "I've missed you."

Tierra blew warm breath past her parted lips. "I missed you, too," she whispered, as she suddenly leaned up to meet his mouth with her own.

Travis dropped deep into the kiss, emotion swelling thick and full from his spirit. He'd been dreaming about kissing her since that first time, and now here she was, wanting him to kiss her again. His lips danced with hers, moving in perfect sync. It felt like an eternity before either of them broke the connection, the sweetness of it too beautiful to let go of.

"I'm sorry," Tierra said, panting ever so slightly. "I was scared."

Travis nodded. "You don't need to be scared, Tierra.

I will do whatever it takes to prove to you how much I love you."

"Is it really love?" Tierra closed her eyes, shaking her head as she tried to take everything in. She was suddenly on emotional overload. "I don't know what it is I'm feeling," she said softly, her gaze meeting his evenly as she reopened her eyes.

Travis nodded. "There's nothing wrong with that, Tierra. You've been through a lot, and this is happening very fast."

She nodded. "Too fast. That's why it's petrifying me," she said, turning to eye the space around her.

The open-air enclosure was more than she'd expected with its queen-size bed canopied in mosquito netting and sheer white linens. Two wicker chairs adorned the corner. With the exception of there being no windows or doors, the spot was very romantic with its soft decor and the natural foliage surrounding it.

"This is pretty," she said, changing the subject.

Travis chuckled. "If you say so. I figured you'd be more comfortable here than in a sleeping bag down on the ground."

She giggled with him. "I guess it's pretty obvious that I'm really not the outdoorsy type."

"A little." Travis stepped in behind her and pressed his hands to her shoulders. "There's a bathroom with a shower on the other side of the sky bridge there," he said, gesturing with his head.

"Thank goodness for that," Tierra said with a slight laugh, suddenly unnerved by the nearness of him. She loved his hands against her skin, the appendages so strong and firm, yet soft and gentle at the same time. She gave in to the sensations sweeping through her spirit, relaxing back against his broad chest.

Travis continued to caress her shoulders and the length of her arms. "You're so tense," he said, muttering softly against her ear.

Tierra didn't answer, unable to form any coherent words. She wasn't ready yet for what was starting to happen between them. But she didn't want to push him away again, either.

"Hey," she said, trying to sound casual. "Can a girl get a tour?"

Travis nodded his understanding. He was feeling it, too, sensing Tierra's rising discomfort. He didn't want her to be afraid to be with him. When it was right, she would want it as much as he did. He wanted her to want him just as much.

He clasped her hand in his, leading her back to the landing platform. "Grab your helmet," he said easily. "Let's go picnic by the lake."

When the morning sun rose, Tierra was sleeping soundly against the padded mattress, still fully clothed in her jeans and T-shirt. Just as Travis had suggested, they'd gone down to the lakeside for a picnic lunch. Travis had paid some of the staff to go get them sandwiches from a nearby shop. Ham and cheese on whole-wheat bread with orange soda had filled their stomachs nicely.

The rest of the afternoon had been spent swimming, fishing, canoeing, hiking and exerting every ounce of energy the two could muster. Just as dusk began to darken the sky, the two had zipped back to the tree house. When Travis had disappeared to go take a shower,

Tierra had lain across the bed and had fallen straight to sleep.

Staring down at her, Travis couldn't help but marvel at how exquisitely beautiful she was. She looked like an angel as she slumbered so peacefully. He hadn't been able to sleep as soundly. His desire had been pandemic, his wanting rampant with her being so near to him.

He'd found her dozing when he'd come back from the showers and he hadn't wanted to disturb her. The air mattress they kept stored beneath the bed gave him something soft to sleep on without disturbing Tierra's rest. But not even the sounds of the night creatures had moved her. Raccoons and ringtails had moved about outside the space, and Tierra hadn't budged. A local coyote had sung to the moon and resident screech owls and great horned owls had serenaded them, and still she hadn't moved. Even now, as the early morning calls of the birds and the trickle of the waterfall in the distance rippled through the air, Tierra dozed easily.

But Travis had heard them all, tossing and turning as sleep had eluded him. Through the night he had wanted nothing more than to be able to crawl into the bed beside her, strip them both out of their clothes and make passionate love the whole night long. His morning erection still lingered at the thought.

Tierra could barely remember returning to the room, and falling asleep across the bed was a complete befuddlement to her. She hadn't heard the man moving quietly around her, but right then she felt his hands gently caressing her back. His touch felt good as he ran his fingertips up her spine, along her shoulder blades and over her shoulders. Unable to resist, she moaned, a soft mutter muffled by the pillow beneath her head. As he brushed the length of her hair aside, Travis leaned to plant a damp kiss against the back of her neck.

"Hey, sleepyhead, are you planning to stay here all day?"

Tierra smiled, her eyes still closed tightly. The fresh morning air tickled her nostrils as she took a deep inhale of air. "Good morning!"

"Good morning to you. It's time to get up."

Tierra hummed softly. "Hmmmm. I don't want to."

Chuckling, Travis tapped her buttocks. "Let's move it, princess. The fish are biting and we need to catch dinner."

Tierra groaned. "No fishing!"

Laughing, Travis dropped down onto the bed beside her, his hands still skating across her back and shoulders. He leaned to kiss the top of her head. "Well then, we'll just do some hiking. There's a lot to explore in these here hills!"

"What's so wrong with room service and shopping?" she asked teasingly. "I can do shopping."

Travis laughed again, the wealth of it filling the morning air. "There's no room service here, and definitely no shopping. Now, are you going to get up and get a shower by yourself, or am I going to put you in the shower?"

Tierra opened her eyes and looked up at him. Her mind was suddenly running rampant with the possibilities. Their afternoon together had been one of the best experiences she'd had in a very long time. Tierra had gotten to see another side of Travis, his conservative nature more casual and relaxed. He'd also gotten to see a side of her that she herself had never experienced. The entire day had been challenging, moving her to do things she would never have imagined doing before.

They had talked for hours, conversation flowing as easily as the flow of water that rippled across the lake. They'd laughed, and once or twice she had teared up with emotion. Even the moments of silence had been easy and relaxed, allowing them both to discover comfort in just being quiet with each other.

Tierra had allowed herself to fantasize about the man, imagining the promise of him and her together. She had thought the night would have gone differently. She hadn't given any thought to her falling asleep without the two of them exploring more of their relationship. But she had, and he had allowed her that time to herself. There had been no expectations, no demands, nothing she wasn't totally and completely comfortable with.

Tierra could no longer deny the attraction she had for him. Nor could she deny that what she was feeling was so much more about who he was and how he was than just the heat he ignited deep in her feminine spirit. She was feeling something for the man that couldn't be refuted or ignored.

She shifted her body until she was lying on her side facing him. "I imagine, Mr. Stallion, that you and I in a shower will have a very different ending from the last time we found ourselves in that position."

Tierra sat upright, her voice dropping to a sultry whisper. "I also imagine that if that happens, we won't be doing any fishing or shopping today." She looked him directly in the eye, reaching out her hand and dropping it against his knee. She slowly caressed his thick thigh.

The gesture sent a bolt of electricity straight through the man. Travis met her gaze. "So, you decide," he whispered back. "Are you taking your shower with my assistance, or are you going to do it all by your lonesome?"

Tierra smiled, her lips bending slowly. Travis Stallion had haunted her dreams, walking in and out of her sleep. Their day together had been exhausting, and even as she'd drifted off into a deep sleep she couldn't help but imagine the two of them making sweet love together. She wanted him to make love to her. She wanted him right then and there.

Rising from the bed, Tierra continued to watch him as he watched her. She kicked off her sneakers and socks as she slowly lifted her T-shirt up and over her head. Reaching both hands behind her, she unsnapped her white lace bra and let it fall to the floor beneath her feet. Travis's eyes widened as he gasped, awed by the beauty of her.

Turning from him, Tierra headed across the planked floor to the bridge that swung between the bedroom and the bathroom. Travis had risen, standing by the bedside as he stared after her.

"I'll need someone to help me wash my back," she said, tossing him a glance over her shoulder. And then she eased her way across the sky bridge, sunshine lighting her path as her naked backside beckoned him to follow.

Chapter 14

The shower enclosure was small, much smaller than the shower they'd shared at the Stallion family home. By the time Travis made his way to her side, he was as naked as she was, his clothes abandoned along the short walkway.

Stepping into the flow of heated water, Travis pressed his hands to her shoulders, moving his body close to hers. His fingers skated down the length of her arms, tickling her flesh. Tierra closed her eyes as he moved against her, her back and buttocks kissing his chest and thighs. A shiver raced from the pit of her stomach down and out into her limbs. She was enjoying a delightful throb between her legs. The rush she'd gotten from exposing herself to him didn't begin to compare to the sexy feeling now shimmering deep in her stomach.

Reaching for a bar of soap, Travis rubbed lather between his hands and then drew his palms across her body. He soaped and massaged her back first, relieving the last ounce of tension that had accumulated there. Tierra moaned in pleasure, a sigh of contentment blowing past her lips. "That really feels nice," she said softly.

She suddenly gasped in surprise as Travis's hands skated across her buttocks, kneading her cheeks. The gesture made her giggle softly. Travis laughed with her.

"You've got a nice rear view," Travis murmured into her ear. "A very nice rear view."

Tierra turned in his arms, moving him to wrap them around her torso. She hugged him back, clasping her hands together at the small of his back. She pressed her breasts tight against his torso. The sensation of his skin against hers teased her nipples until they were rock-candy hard, standing at full attention.

Travis continued to lavish her with suds, his hands and soap gliding effortlessly over her body. When he reached for her breasts, caressing one and then the other, she knew there would be no turning back. She was suddenly excited at the prospect of their growing relationship taking them where neither had gone before.

Tilting her face to his, Tierra kissed him. Their lips touched first, then their tongues, meeting like old friends for the first time. Their passion rose in intensity, her tongue eagerly searching his mouth, reaching for the back of his throat. Travis moaned as Tierra danced in his mouth and gently sucked on his lips. He couldn't remember having ever tasted anything so sweet.

Travis trailed a path of kisses from her mouth down her chin to her neck, nibbling his way back to her mouth again. His hands were racing from one point on her body to another, not wanting to stop nor knowing where to move next. He was being consumed by his want of the woman, his taut muscles about to explode with pleasure.

Tierra opened her eyes wide, staring deep into his. In that moment, she couldn't begin to imagine what her life might be like without him. More important, she knew she didn't want to. "I want you," Tierra muttered before kissing his mouth again.

Nodding his understanding Travis eased a large hand between her thighs, his fingers teasing the line of her secret treasure. He pressed the pad of his thumb against the button that had swelled full, eager for his attention. Tierra's body suddenly spasmed with pleasure.

Moisture ran from the showerhead above them, mixing with the moisture that dripped against his hand. Tierra purred, consumed by the rapture sweeping through her. Wanting more, she reached her hand between their two bodies, eagerly wrapping her fingers around the length of his manhood. Steel pulsed against her palm, the length of him expanding even more as she slowly began to stroke him back and forth. With each stroke, she was unconsciously moving her hips against him, grinding her pelvis hard against his leg.

Travis dropped both of his hands to her waist and lifted her off her feet. He pressed her body against the shower wall as Tierra wrapped her legs around his pelvis and her arms around his neck. She kissed his mouth as the length of his erection pressed teasingly at the door of her feminine spot.

Tierra's touch had him on sensory overload. It was

taking all of Travis's fortitude not to explode right then and there from the pleasure. The wanting made him whimper ever so softly.

Sweeping her into his arms, Travis carried her from the shower back to the bedroom. Around them the sun had risen full and bright in the deep blue sky, light glistening through the trees around them. Laying her down against the comforter, Travis stepped back to admire the view.

He'd never known a woman more beautiful. Her damp skin glistened in the daylight. The luxurious mane of hair was splayed above her head, framing her face. Travis sucked in a quick gasp of air as Tierra opened her legs widely, one manicured hand gliding across her breasts as the other stopped at the cusp of her pubic hair. In that moment, the desire she had for him was spilling like a tidal wave out of her large brown eyes.

He moved to his overnight bag, searching a zippered compartment until he found a foil-wrapped condom hidden inside. As he made his way back to the bedside, he tore the wrapper with his teeth.

Tierra leaned up on her elbows, watching as he eased the prophylactic over his engorged member. Lust flooded his expression, his desire flashing like a neon sign.

Reclining back against the bed, Tierra splayed her legs wide open. Travis dropped his body down against hers, pressing his lips back to her lips. She gasped loudly as Travis eased himself slowly into her. The moment was surreal as Tierra welcomed him inside, thrusting her body eagerly against his.

Travis clasped her face between his palms, his stare penetrating hers. His body moved against her body,

Tierra meeting him thrust for thrust. The moment was overwhelming and tears suddenly pooled behind Tierra's eyelids. No man had ever loved her so sweetly. Never before had her body been so in sync with someone else's. The couple was panting and gasping in unison, both frenzied with desire.

Travis felt himself edging closer to that moment of bliss. He could tell by Tierra's expression that she was ready to fall over that edge with him. He moaned her name over and over again as if in prayer, and Tierra answered him with an entreaty of her own. Wrapping her legs around his buttocks, she clutched his back, her nails barely digging into his bare flesh.

Like two perfectly tuned instruments, the couple played each other beautifully. The music between them was an opus of desire and yearning, orchestrated with masterful precision. Neither had known it possible to create such a work of art without even trying.

When he exploded, spilling himself into her, Tierra cried out loudly, his name rolling like melted butter from her tongue as she climaxed with him. She cried out his name and showed Travis that she loved him, too.

Tierra would not be moved from where she lay. She was spent, her body completely exhausted. She and Travis had made love over and over again, the man's stamina limitless. By late afternoon, hunger had gotten the best of them both.

"We could ride into town for some supper," Travis suggested, lying on his side, his body spooning hers.

"We could," Tierra responded. "But I don't have any

desire to get up," she admitted. She rocked her buttocks against his pelvis.

Travis chuckled. "You just don't want to zip back down to the gates."

"That, too!"

The man moved against her, a flicker of energy pulsing ever so slightly through his groin. "I guess I could zip down by myself and bring us something back."

Rolling against him, Tierra pressed herself against his body. His skin was still damp from perspiration, sweat moistening his skin. "That actually sounds like it would be a very good idea," she said, pressing a gentle kiss between his breast bone.

A deep smile pulled at Travis's mouth as he eased his hands through her hair and kissed her back, pressing his lips to her forehead. He lifted his body from the bed and reached for his clothes, pulling his jeans and tank back on. He slipped his large feet into his boots and adjusted the belt around his waist.

"Do you want something in particular?" Travis queried, amusement painting his expression.

Tierra shrugged nonchalantly. "Filet mignon, lobster tail and chocolate mousse for dessert."

The man chuckled. "Two burgers and fries coming right up, Ms. Braddy."

Tierra laughed. "Don't forget the chocolate."

"And a side of moon pie!" Travis exclaimed.

Stepping into his harness and adjusting his helmet, Travis moved to the outside landing. Peering back into the room, he called out Tierra's name.

"Yes?"

"Baby, I miss you already," the man said before casting himself down the zip line.

Tierra's words echoed behind him. "I miss you more, sweetheart!"

Tierra woke to the sound of rain tapping against the leaves on the trees. The gentle patter was soothing as moisture dripped and puddled down to the ravine below. Except for the splatter of raindrops, all else was quiet outside, nothing seeming to move at all through the trees.

A cool breeze blew gently, the temperature having dropped considerably from the afternoon heat. A night-light plugged into the far wall illuminated the space, and a small moth fluttered back and forth in front of it. The tranquil environment was nothing like Tierra could have imagined herself enjoying.

Travis lay beside her, sleeping peacefully. The man had exhausted every ounce of his energy. Tierra had lost count of the number of times they'd pleasured each other, no corner of the room missed as they'd moved from the bed to the floor and back again. They'd made love in the shower twice, her back pressed against the shower stall, her legs wrapped around his waist as Travis had pulled and pushed her body against his. They had fallen asleep wrapped in each other's arms, and even now, as Tierra lay wide awake beside him, Travis was draped around her like a warm blanket.

As if he sensed her no longer sleeping, Travis nuzzled his face into her neck. "Why aren't you asleep? Aren't you tired?" he muttered against her skin.

"I was dreaming about you, and it woke me up," she answered sweetly.

"What were you dreaming?"

"We were old and gray and at our daughter's wedding."

The man smiled sheepishly. "Was she as beautiful a bride as her mother? Because you know her mother is going to be a beautiful bride."

Tierra smiled. "You don't quit, do you?"

"Should I? I mean really, do you want me to?"

Tierra blew warm air past her lips. She snuggled down closer to the man. "Would it hurt your feelings if I told you I don't know what I want?"

Travis wrapped his arms tightly around her, hugging her against him. "It would hurt my feelings more if you weren't honest with me."

She brushed her head against his chest. "What I do know is that you have made the last couple of weeks absolutely incredible, even when you were being annoying. I know that you make me laugh, and when I'm with you I feel safe and secure. I know that when you took off I missed you terribly. And I know that right now, being with you here, like this, means more to me than I would have ever expected. That's what I do know."

Travis nuzzled his face into her hair, gently kissing the top of her head. Tierra turned in his arms and touched her lips to his. "And I also know that if I had to marry any man, right now, I think you would be the man I would want to spend the rest of my life with."

Travis chuckled. "I think I like what you know! So, finish telling me about our daughter and her wedding."

* * *

As Travis stepped out of the shower, he was grinning from ear to ear. He couldn't begin to explain how incredible he was feeling. They were scheduled to check out before noon and head back to Dallas, but truth be told, he didn't want to leave. A part of him was afraid that if they did, the magic they were feeling in this place might disappear and move them back to the place where Tierra wanted to push him away instead of holding him close to her.

He grinned as she eased into the room, slipping past him into the downpour of water that sprinkled from the showerhead.

"It's cold!" Tierra exclaimed.

Travis laughed. "I told you to get up and get into the shower with me."

"I needed a few more minutes of sleep. You could have saved me some hot water."

Travis laughed. "Are you pouting?"

"Yes," Tierra said as she stepped out of the spray of water and reached for a plush towel.

Travis was brushing his teeth in front of the sink. He passed her a toothbrush coated with mint-flavored toothpaste. They stood side by side polishing their enamel, brushing and rinsing with mouthwash. Tierra passed him a washcloth to wipe his mouth. As they stared at each other in the mirror, she leaned her head against his shoulder.

"I leave next week, Tierra. I have to report back to base by Friday."

Tierra entwined her fingers between his. She nodded. "I know."

They exhaled heavily at the same time.

Moving back into the other room, neither said another word. Reaching the bed, Travis pressed a kiss to her shoulder, his hands snaking around her abdomen and up to her breasts. His rising erection pressed eagerly against her back. He kissed her neck and her shoulders.

Bending her forward, Travis caressed her buttocks, squeezing one cheek and then the other. Dropping to his knees, he kissed the small of her back, drawing his tongue across the curve of her behind. When he softly nibbled the lush tissue, slowly suckling a love bite against her flesh, Tierra wiggled from side to side, her excitement mounting.

She laughed. "You're going to leave a mark," she whispered huskily.

Travis grinned. "Good, that way everyone will know you belong to me," he answered as he continued to tease her.

When his fingers slipped down between her legs, tickling her most private spot, Tierra gasped loudly, clutching the bed for support. Travis fingered her gently, teasing and taunting her feminine core. She moaned his name, biting her lower lip as waves of pleasure swept through her.

"You are so sexy!" Travis exclaimed. He pushed her gently, rolling her onto her back.

Air caught tight in Tierra's chest as Travis trailed a path of damp kisses against her inner thighs. Meeting his gaze, Tierra felt her body pleading for him to touch her, to taste the sweetness of her honey. As he drew closer, Tierra's body arched upward, eager to experience his intimate kiss.

When his mouth touched her, his tongue eagerly searching the petals of her secret garden, Tierra bit her lower lip again to stifle a loud moan. Her dark eyes were clouded with desire. As she moved her hips against him, Travis knew she was close, her body ready to explode.

He moved his ministrations up her abdomen, his tongue slipping in and out of her belly button. Reaching her breasts, he suckled one nipple and then the other, kneading the handful of flesh eagerly. Reaching for a condom on the nightstand, Travis sheathed himself quickly, then plunged his body into hers.

Dropping his weight against her, Travis eased his left arm around her neck, his cheek pressed tight to her cheek. His right hand reached down to the back of her thigh, lifting her leg around his back as he moved himself in and out of her slowly and then faster and harder as his own excitement mounted. Tierra met him stroke for stroke, every nerve ending in her body screaming for release.

Relief came quickly, their worlds exploding into a million pieces, ecstasy spreading through both their bodies as waves of pleasure washed over them. Lying side by side, the moment couldn't have been more perfect.

Chapter 15

He had been eyeing the buxom blonde and her red-headed friend like they were both meat on a hook. The two young women giggled foolishly at the attention he had been showing them, both women captivated by the soldier in uniform.

Damien Porter had turned on the charm during their layover at Chicago's O'Hare International Airport and was still going strong by the time they'd reached Dallas/Fort Worth. When the redhead had gestured for him to follow her into the plane's restroom, her friend sound asleep in the seat beside them, Damien had followed willingly.

Stepping out of the terminal, Damien had programmed both telephone numbers into his cell phone, promising to give each a call the first chance he got. He'd winked at the redhead and had blown the blonde a kiss after hailing himself a taxicab and waving goodbye.

Glancing at the watch on his wrist, Damien now debated whether or not he should call Tierra and let her know he was coming. After much thought, he decided not to, thinking he would be better served if he surprised her instead.

The man peered out the taxi window. It felt like it had been forever since he'd last been home to Dallas. He thought he would have missed it, but he hadn't. He hadn't missed anything or anyone.

The taxi driver eyed him curiously, striking up a conversation. "So, you home for a while, soldier?"

Damien shrugged. "Nah, just a few days. Need to handle some business is all, then I'm back to the front lines."

"I don't envy you guys over there. I know y'all is doing some hard work. We really appreciate it."

"Oh, yeah, thanks," Damien said.

"You got family here?" the man asked.

Damien nodded. "My girl is here."

"Oh, you're married? You got any kids?"

Damien laughed. "No, dude. Not yet, at least. I was hoping to stay single, but you know how it is. Sometimes we got to play the game to keep them hanging on the line. This one's a keeper. She'll do anything for you while you get to do whatever you want to do for yourself."

The driver laughed with him. "So, it's like that!"

"Yeah, man. It's like that!"

And it was like that, Damien thought, falling back into self-reflection. He'd had Tierra on a thin leash since forever. He'd lost count of the promises he'd made to her and had broken, the girl forgiving him each and every time. Tierra was good like that.

Damien knew that Tierra loved him. He wished he could return the favor, but he had to admit he didn't love anyone but himself. Women were a dime a dozen, falling all over him as the moment moved them. He couldn't help that he sometimes needed to catch one or two to soften their landing when they fell head over heels for him.

Damien had to be honest and admit that he just liked women. He liked a lot of them, and he wasn't ready to settle down with just one. It just wasn't always necessary to admit it to other people. What Tierra didn't know wouldn't hurt either one of them.

The last fling he'd tapped had come closer to moving his heart than anyone, even moving him to break off his engagement to Tierra. Then he'd made that pit stop in London, meeting the tall, thin Jamaican sister who'd turned his head, and he just couldn't help himself. His fling hadn't been happy about that indiscretion. Women were so sensitive about the damndest things, Damien thought.

Now he was regretting his breakup with Tierra. The two of them had worked out a nice arrangement. He was certain Tea would give him another chance. He'd turn on the charm, sweet talk her out of her clothes and work that magic while he got himself a taste of her goodies. Then he would tell her how much he loved and missed her and be back in before he could blink an eye. Tierra was a sure thing like that.

At least Damien was hoping so. Uncertainty furled his brow. He had at least expected her to call and try to talk him into taking her back. But she hadn't. He'd not heard a single word from her, and she hadn't returned one of his calls. Maybe she had finally gotten over him. Damien grunted. *That wasn't likely,* he thought, his mouth bending into a knowing smile. Damien was sure of his magnetism if he wasn't sure of anything else.

What was most important, though, was finding out what Tierra had done with the money in their joint account. When he had tried to access those funds, the bank had advised him that his name had been removed from the account. Since it was highly unusual for any woman to beat him to the punch, Damien had figured a quick trip home to resolve the matter was in definite order. And if Tierra wasn't willing to play his way, he might as well get his engagement ring back, too. He'd dropped a pretty penny on that thing to just walk away without demanding she return it to him.

Shifting in his seat as the driver navigated traffic, Damien crossed his arms over his chest. He wasn't so concerned. Like he'd often thought before, Tierra was a sure thing like that. And he always bet on a sure thing.

The front door opening and then closing pulled Damien out of a sound sleep. Tierra hadn't been home when he'd arrived, and he'd been sitting around for two whole days trying to figure out where she was. He needed to get her straight about her comings and goings, he thought, as he rose from where he'd fallen asleep on the sofa. He suddenly cringed when he heard the matriarch's deep voice calling out his name.

"Boy, what are you doing in my child's house?" Mama Dee said, her voice rising.

Damien wiped at the sleep in his eyes, suddenly wishing he could wake up from what was sure to be a nightmare.

"I'm not going to ask you again," Mama Dee said, her hands gripping the sides of her hips. "When did you get into town, and why are you here?"

"Good morning, Mama Dee. I was just waiting here for Tierra. Do you know where she is?"

The old woman's stare was chilling. Behind her, Tingin Braddy stood with his arms crossed over his torso, taking it all in. Damien flipped his hand in a quick wave. Tingin gestured with his head in response.

Mama Dee responded. "Damien, I don't think Tierra is your concern anymore, son. In fact, I know my grandbaby is no concern of yours."

"Mama Dee, I made a huge mistake, but I was scared. I'm here hoping Tierra will forgive me." Damien's look was pleading.

Tierra's grandmother continued to eye him with reservation. After a few quick minutes she directed her comments to her grandson.

"Tingin, put those containers in the refrigerator, baby. I don't want that food to spoil. Then just go check the back rooms. Make sure Tierra's stuff is where it's supposed to be."

Mama Dee cut her eye at Damien. Moving to the upholstered wing chair that rested across from where he sat on the sofa, she took a seat, still staring at the man. Damien couldn't help but wish he could drop into a hole and disappear, or, even better, throw the old woman into a hole and make her disappear.

"Mama Dee, I'm very sorry," he started, prepared to plead his case.

The woman held up her hand, stalling his words. She slowly crossed one leg over the other as she leaned back in her seat. Her stare was still focused on Damien, the look she was giving him like a dagger gutting him from stem to stern. He knew, though, that he was going to have to sit quietly through whatever it was she was planning to dish out to him. He also knew that he'd have to get Mama Dee to consider forgiving him if he had even half a chance to reconcile with Tierra.

The matriarch cleared her throat before she began speaking. "Damien, son, I'm not sure why you're here. I imagine, though, that Tierra has something you must want real bad."

"No, really, Mama—"

The look she gave him made him bite back his words. Contrition painted his expression, and he apologized for interrupting.

Mama Dee continued. "I'm sure you want something, Damien. Since you were a little boy you rarely did anything that didn't benefit you first and everyone else last. You've always been selfish like that.

"I don't have to tell you that I'm not at all happy with you. And Tierra knows that I do not support this relationship. She deserves better than you, Damien. She deserves so much more. You're still a little boy trying to be a little boy. Tierra needs herself a good man, and there is nothing good about you, child."

Mama Dee paused, allowing her words to settle against Damien's ears. She stood back up as she finished. "Tierra will be home later this afternoon. And I imagine that you two will probably have a lot to talk about. And when that conversation is over, I really want you to try and do better, Damien. I know you can do better. The next woman who comes into your life will want that from you."

Damien came to his feet, drawing his hands up and down against the wrinkled pants he'd slept in. "I think Tierra and I can make this work, Mama Dee. I want to be a better man for her."

Mama Dee laughed, shaking her head. "Boy, you just don't have a clue," she said, moving back to the front door. "Good luck, Damien. Whatever the future has for you, I wish you much good luck."

Gesturing her head in Tingin's direction, Mama Dee pointed her finger at her grandchild. "Tierra should be here in the next hour or so. You need to stay until she gets back. Make sure he don't take nothin' that doesn't belong to him," she said as she adjusted her sweater around her shoulders.

As the front door closed behind her, Tingin turned toward his former friend, his two fists clutched tightly at his sides. "You know you've got a beat-down coming, right?"

Damien held up both hands, a cautious air falling over his shoulders. "Hey, dude, let's not do this. No harm, no foul, right?"

Tingin shook his head as he took another step closer. "It would give me great pleasure to hurt you, but I don't have to. You've used my sister for the last time. I think Tierra's got a thing or two planned for you, buddy boy!"

Damien shrugged. "I don't know what Tierra told you, but—"

Tingin interrupted the man. "Brother, you need to just sit down and shut up before I lose all of my patience. Hitting you might make me feel better, but it won't change anything, so if you don't talk, the chances that I won't slam my fist into your face are in your favor."

Rolling his eyes, Damien sat back down. Right now he needed to focus on carrying through with his plans for Tierra. He'd make things right with Tingin some other time.

The trip back to Dallas had been quiet, the duo reveling in the silence. As the Stallion family jet landed safely on the airstrip, Travis and Tierra met each other's gaze. Their extended getaway was officially over. A limousine sat in wait at the end of the tarmac, the driver gesturing in their direction as they made their way down the airplane's steps.

Travis greeted the man warmly. "Good afternoon, Mr. Landry."

"Mr. Stallion, sir. Welcome back. Good day, Ms. Braddy," the Stallions' long-time driver said with a slight gesture of his head.

Tierra smiled sweetly, the gesture brightening her face. "Hi!"

"Will you two be returning to the ranch, sir?"

Travis looked toward Tierra. "We're actually going to Ms. Braddy's apartment, Mr. Landry." He gave the man the address.

"Yes, sir."

Inside the vehicle, the two held hands. The conversation was limited, polite chitchat filling the emptiness. Nervous tension seemed to rise out of nowhere, wrapping them tightly in an awkward embrace.

"So, what now?" Tierra finally asked.

"I wasn't kidding when I said I wanted to marry you, Tierra. I want you to be my wife, and I want that to happen before I have to report back to Afghanistan. We just need to figure out how to make that happen."

Tierra nodded her head slowly, an easy sigh slipping out of her mouth. She met his intense stare, searching for the answers to her future in his eyes. She nodded slowly. "I… We…" she stammered, the right words seeming to elude her. She took a deep breath. "Can we please talk about this later," she whispered. "Please?"

Travis squeezed her hand beneath his, no other words needed to assure her that when she was ready, he would be, as well.

The limo stopped short in front of her apartment building. Tierra flashed him a wide smile despite the confusion that was still swimming in her head.

As the driver opened the door to let them out, Tierra leaned to kiss Travis's cheek. "You're still coming up, aren't you, Sergeant Stallion?"

The man smiled. "Yes, ma'am, of course I am!"

Arm in arm, the two moved from the building's lobby into the elevator and up to the twenty-second floor. Laughter had risen easily, pushing their earlier anxiety away. Just as Tierra was searching the bottom of her handbag for her keys, the front door swung open, her brother standing on the other side. Startled, the couple both stared.

"Hey!" Tierra exclaimed, the surprise registered in her voice. "What are you doing here?"

Tingin Braddy smiled weakly. "Hey." He met Travis's questioning stare, extending his hand in greeting. "Hi, I'm Tingin Braddy, Tierra's brother."

"Hi, Travis Stallion," the man said, shaking the hand that had been offered to him.

"What are you doing here?" Tierra asked again, concern suddenly washing over her face.

"Mama Dee and I stopped by to check on the place like you wanted. She asked me to stay until you got back."

"Is something wrong, Tingin? Mama Dee's fine, isn't she?"

"Oh, yeah," Tingin answered. "She's good. But when we got here we found—"

The man's comment was suddenly interrupted, a voice coming from behind him.

"He found me here waiting for you, Tea." Damien Porter stepped up behind her brother, a broad grin across his face.

"Damien?" Tierra's expression was incredulous, disbelief blanketing her face. She was suddenly acutely aware of Travis's hand pressed against the small of her back.

Pushing his way past Tingin, Damien swept Tierra up into his arms. "I'm so sorry, sweetheart. I don't know what got into me, but I realize I made a horrible mistake. I love you, Tea, and I just had to come and try to make things right between us."

Chapter 16

The two men pulled up to the bar, Tingin gesturing for the bartender.

"What'll you have?" the burly, red-faced man asked, wiping down the oak structure with a damp rag.

"Two shots of Jack Daniels."

"With two beer chasers," Travis added, holding up two fingers and waving them in the air.

The bartender nodded, moving to prep their drinks.

"Well, it's nice to officially meet you," Tingin said, cutting his eye in Travis's direction. "Mama Dee's had a lot to say about you."

Travis smiled. "She's a sweetheart."

Tingin nodded. "She has her moments."

"That's what your sister said." Travis chuckled.

Both men paused as their two shots were dropped onto the counter in front of them. With a quick clink of their glasses, they tilted back their heads and downed the umber-colored fluid in one swallow.

"We'll do that one more time," Travis said as he pulled two twenty-dollar bills from his pocket and passed them to the man. "Thank you."

Both men blew a deep sigh at the same time.

"Well, isn't this something," Travis said, reaching for conversation.

The other man nodded. "It's a mess, is what it is."

Travis nodded, not knowing what else there was for him to say. Mess didn't begin to define what the situation had turned into.

Tierra had been visibly shaken to have Damien Porter standing in her living room. Travis had wanted nothing more than to be able to console her, to assure her that things would be just fine. But he knew that wasn't something he could promise the woman. In that moment, nothing had felt fine. And then he realized that him being there, after having spent the weekend with her, had only made the situation even more awkward.

Damien hadn't given anyone else much opportunity to say anything, chattering a mile per minute trying to explain himself to Tierra. It hadn't registered with the man at all that she and Travis had been together, arriving at her home at the same time.

It had been Tingin who'd suggested that the two of them walk down the block to the bar for a drink to give Tierra and Damien time alone to talk. Travis hadn't been much interested in giving them time alone for anything at all. The look on Tierra's face had been daunting, the woman clearly feeling besieged by it all. Now all he wanted was to be back in Tierra's living room staking his claim on the woman's heart.

Tingin sensed his unease. "Hey, I'm sure Tea's giving Damien his walking papers as we speak. There is no way she'd ever consider taking him back after everything he's done to her. My sister's way too smart for that."

"Your sister has been on an emotional roller coaster for the past few weeks. There's no telling what she might do."

Another awkward silence settled over the duo. Travis twisted the chilled bottle of beer between his hands, palming it nervously.

"You really care about my sister, don't you?" Tingin asked, cutting his eye at the man a second time.

His question cut through the thick silence that had filled the space between them. Travis turned to look the man in his eyes.

"Let me tell you a story," Travis said. He continued to twirl his bottle of beer as he turned in his seat to face the man. "Do you remember the Yearwood Center that used to be down on Lafayette Street?"

"Yeah, we spent a few summers there. They had a great kids program."

Travis nodded his agreement. "I was fourteen years old the summer I went. I'd come to Texas to visit with my cousins. It was the year before my aunt and uncle were killed, and they sent us there for the summer basketball program."

"I played basketball," Tingin exclaimed excitedly. "Coach Tolliver was the coach!"

"Coach Tolliver was in charge," Travis said at the same time.

A wide grin spread across both their faces. Tingin laughed. “So we were probably there at the same time.”

“The year I was there, the girls use to cheer for the teams. There was this one skinny little girl who wore the same striped red-and-yellow socks for every game.”

Tingin burst out laughing, the sound rising from deep in his gut. “Oh, say it’s not so!”

“One day I scored the winning basket, and out of nowhere she came running over and hugged me. She was the littlest thing with the biggest, brightest eyes. I have never forgotten your sister’s eyes. She still has the most beautiful eyes.”

Tingin was still laughing. “Does Tierra know?”

Travis shook his head. “No. I haven’t told her yet.”

The two men lifted their bottles of beer and took sips at the same time. For a few quick moments they sat in quiet reflection, both amused by just how small a world it was.

“And I do care about Tierra. Even more than she realizes. I’ve fallen in love with your sister,” he said, finally answering Tingin’s original question. The conviction of his statement left no doubt in Tingin’s mind as the man repeated himself. “I love her very much.”

“Damn,” Tingin muttered. He took a swig of his beer.

“What’s wrong?” Travis questioned.

“I don’t mind having your back, brother. We’ll do whatever we need to do. To tell you the truth, I would really like to body-slam Damien into a deep hole, but hey, if we can toss him out peacefully, I’ll go for that.

“And for the record, I had my money on Tierra being

an old maid until she was fifty, and you had to come along and throw off my odds."

Travis laughed. "Sorry, guy, but that's one bet you have definitely lost." He tapped the neck of his beer bottle against Tingin's. "I have no intentions of letting your sister stay single past next week."

"Y'all are all crazy!"

"Love will do that to you."

Tierra's big brother nodded slowly. Then he changed the subject. "You do play golf, right?"

"I do."

"And you hunt, fish, bowl…?"

Travis laughed. "Yes, sir, I do it all."

"You, I like!" Tingin gestured for one more refill. "Drink up. If we have to carry Damien out ourselves, he's being permanently evicted tonight."

Travis chugged the last of his drink. "My future brother-in-law, I like how you think!"

Tierra had been locked in her bedroom for over an hour, Damien standing outside the door pleading his case. She couldn't begin to fathom how she'd gotten herself into such a situation. Confusion was clearly weighing down her spirit.

For the life of her she couldn't understand why Tingin and Travis had left her. There was absolutely nothing she wanted to discuss with Damien. All she wanted was for him to collect the last of his personal possessions and go as far from her sight as he could.

Damien tapped against the door for the umpteenth time, calling out her name. "Tierra, baby, please," he whined.

She rolled her eyes skyward, shaking her head. "What?"

"Please, baby, we have to talk about this."

"No, Damien, we really don't. You said everything you had to say in your letter. There is no need for conversation now."

"I was confused, Tierra. And scared."

"I was scared, too, Damien, but you didn't see me finding someone else to make me happy. Isn't that what you wrote? That you couldn't marry me because you had found someone else?"

"Tierra, open the door. We need to talk, and this is ridiculous. We can't fix this with a door between us."

There was a lengthy moment of silence before the door finally swung wide open. Tierra stood on the other side with a cardboard box in her hand. She shoved the box, and its contents, into Damien's hands.

"There isn't anything between us anymore, Damien. It's over. Now take your stuff and get out of my house! And leave my door keys!" Tierra moved back across the room and took a seat at the foot of the bed. She crossed her arms over her chest, her harsh gaze shooting daggers of ice in the man's direction.

"Baby," Damien continued to plead his case as he set the box down on the floor. He moved to her side, pulling both of her hands into his as he sat down beside her. "Baby, please! I know I messed up, but we can still make this right, Tierra. We can still be married next week before I have to go back to camp. Don't you want that? Don't you want us to be married, Tierra?"

A pregnant pause grew like weeds between them. Tierra's expression was blank, her gaze like ice through the man's heart. "No, Damien," she said finally. "I don't want to marry you. I did once, but not anymore. What I realized, Damien, is that you don't care about anyone except yourself. I thought that if I loved you hard enough you would want to change, but I learned a valuable lesson. You can't change a man. He is who he is, and I don't like who you are."

"But I love you, Tierra, and I know you still love me. Please, Tea!"

Before she could respond, Damien wrapped his arms around her torso and pulled her down to the bed, his mouth pressing eagerly against hers. Tierra's eyes widened at the unexpected kiss, her lips pressed tightly closed as Damien tried to tease her sensibilities. As he tightened his grip, determined to make her remember what she used to feel for him, Tierra pressed both her palms to his chest and pushed.

Standing in the doorway, devastation painted Travis's expression. Tierra lying across her bed kissing Private Porter was not what he'd expected to walk into. As Tingin came down the hallway behind him, the man turned abruptly, fighting the raw emotion threatening to make him do something stupid.

Stepping into the entrance beside his newly minted friend, Tingin gazed where Travis had just stared, his eyes widening with surprise. Tingin met Travis's eyes, noting the hurt that lingered in the man's stare. The glimmer in them had dimmed considerably. He dropped his hand against Travis's shoulder.

As if he'd been burned, Travis snatched his shoulder away. His face was skewed in disappointment. Moving swiftly, Travis pushed past Tingin and made his way back to the front door. Before Tingin could call his name, Travis Stallion was gone.

The palm of Tierra's hand still stung from the slap she'd given Damien. Pushing him from her, she'd slapped his face good, rage rising full steam as she told him in no uncertain terms what she thought about him. Tierra was too through when the man had the audacity to ask her for the money that had been in their joint bank account and her engagement ring back.

"I deserve half that money, Tierra."

"For what, Damien? Breathing? Every dime in that account belongs to me. Consider anything you put into it my severance package. I was a fool to open a joint account with you in the first place, but I corrected that mistake. I have already given you more than you deserve. You won't be taking another blessed thing from me!"

"I'd think you'd want to give me some of it! Why are you being so selfish?"

Tierra's eyes widened harshly, her mind racing. *Selfish? Did he just call me selfish?* "You need to leave, Damien. You need to leave now."

Damien crossed his arms over his chest, taking a hard stand. "What about my ring?"

Tierra laughed. "You gave it to me as a gift, Damien. Since you broke your promise to marry me, I get to keep it. Those are the rules. Consider it my bonus."

"Whose rules?"

"Braddy family rules. Now, get out!"

"Not until you give me what I deserve."

Tierra had something she wanted to give him, all

right, throwing the small lamp that had rested on her nightstand across the room in his direction. The lamp shattered just inches from his head, Damien's eyes widening with fright.

"You crazy witch!" Damien screamed at the top of his lungs.

"I'm going to show you crazy!" Tierra shouted back, reaching for something else heavy to throw.

It was only after Damien had turned tail, pulling his box of possessions back into his hands and dropping her house keys to the floor, that she noticed Tingin standing in the doorway staring at the two of them. As Damien brushed past her brother, Tingin had muttered "good riddance" under his breath, moving to lock the door behind his former friend.

The siblings sat side by side on the chenille sofa. Tears pressed hot against the back of Tierra's eyelids, threatening to spill out of her eyes. Tingin sat strumming his fingers against the side of his leg.

"You okay, Tea?" he finally asked, weary with her silence.

Tierra shook her head.

"Is there anything I can do?"

Tierra continued to shake her head.

Silence again filled the air between them as both stared out into space.

Tingin broke the quiet. "You really should go after him."

Her look was incredulous. "Damien?"

Tingin rolled his eyes at her. "No, Tea, Travis. You need to go after Travis. He clearly misunderstood what he saw."

"He should have trusted me."

"You were kissing another man, for goodness' sake! A man you were engaged to!"

"He still should have had more faith in me."

"Why?"

"Because he knows I love him. He should have trusted that I would never disrespect him or betray his love like that. He knows me."

Tingin leaned forward, his elbows resting atop his thighs as he rested his chin against the back of his folded hands. "Does he, Tierra? I mean, really? Does the man really know that you *love* him? Or has he just been hoping that you might be feeling something for him? Think about it, girl. You two are just getting started with this thing."

Tierra cut her eyes at her brother as he continued.

"Travis met you when you were being dumped by Damien. You and he started hooking up while you were still brokenhearted. Plus you've been fighting his attentions since day one, and that's just the first week with you two. Do you really think he should trust that you love him? Hell, it was only a little while ago you swore you were in love with Damien. Even I might be a little skeptical."

"So what are you saying? You don't think it's possible that I might be in love with Travis?"

Tingin took a deep breath, filling his lungs and then blowing the warm air out quickly. "I'm saying that if you truly love the man you need to go after him. He needs to hear that you weren't kissing your ex-fiancé because you wanted to. If nothing else, Tea, he needs to hear how you feel about Damien suddenly wanting back into your life. And more importantly, he needs to hear you say something about him and you and your relationship."

Tingin sat watching her, allowing his words to seep in and take hold. He rose from his seat, shrugging as he stared down at her. "But hey, that's just my opinion."

"Where are you going?" Tierra asked as her brother crossed to the other side of the room.

"To hang out my shingle… Tingin Braddy, romance therapist at your service."

Tierra shook her head. "I hate you."

Her brother chuckled. "You said hate. I'm gonna tell Mama Dee."

Tierra threw him an indignant look. "I did not."

"Did, too."

She flipped her pinkie finger at him.

"What's that for?"

"People who don't deserve a full salute."

"Girl, you are so stupid!"

Tierra came to her feet, reaching her arms around her brother's waist. She dropped her head against his chest and hugged him tightly. Since they'd been little, her big brother had been her rock, not allowing her to fall too far astray. Whether as a prepubescent tomboy, or the swan she'd evolved into, Tierra had always dived headfirst into everything she endeavored. And when catastrophe hit, Tingin would reel her out to the best of his ability. This time was no exception, her big brother knowing she needed to hear what he had to say.

"I love you, big brother."

Tingin hugged her back. “I love you, too, nuisance. Now please, go find Travis. He fishes, and I want a brother-in-law who fishes.”

Chapter 17

The ride back to the ranch felt like it was taking forever. The concierge at the front desk had hailed a cab for him. Travis sighed, a mournful groan that made the driver eye him curiously in the rearview mirror. Travis tossed a weak smile, his mouth bending ever so slightly. A slight nod of Travis's head moved the man's gaze back to the road in front of him.

Right then, as they sat in midday traffic, Travis was wishing he hadn't sent the limousine back. He would have much preferred the solitude of a backseat with a privacy screen between him and the driver.

It had been too good to be true. Travis couldn't help but think that he had been naive to imagine that he and Tierra could have had a happy ending. But he had been foolish to think that he could have been much more than just a rebound relationship for the woman.

He had truly believed that the two of them could have made things work.

He heaved another deep sigh, his thoughts spinning through his head. There really wasn't any reason for him to stay on in Dallas. He definitely didn't want to be in town while Tierra and Damien headed off to the chapel to make their union legal. Just the thought of Tierra promising herself to that man splintered his heart into a million pieces.

Arriving back at the ranch, Travis was glad that none of his family was around to greet him. As he climbed the front steps and stood in the quiet of the foyer he had no desire to share what had happened with anyone, and the Stallion clan would have had a million and one questions for him to answer. Climbing the stairwell, Travis hurried to his room. Behind the closed door he wouldn't have to pretend that he was okay with anything that had happened.

Tierra was not amused by the taxi driver's humor. The man was making jokes about the midday traffic, and the midday traffic had just about taxed her very last nerve. She tried to fake a smile but she was hardly in the mood to pretend anything. It felt like it was taking forever to get back to Briscoe Ranch.

She'd been playing the entire day over and over again in her head, trying to figure out how things could have gone so incredibly wrong in such a short period of time. Just hours earlier she and Travis had been making love to each other. As they'd landed back in Dallas, she'd been just about ready to commit to them having a future together. Then just like that she wasn't even sure if Travis would even speak to her.

Tierra sank back against the vinyl seat, pulling her fingers through the length of her hair in frustration. The confusion she'd been feeling for the past week had lifted the moment Damien had found his way back home. The moment she'd laid eyes on him she'd known without a degree of doubt that there was nothing left between them. Damien Porter wasn't even a flicker on her heart's radar.

The more Tierra thought about it, the clearer it became that she hadn't been in love with Damien since forever. What she had been enamored with was the idea of being in love. Tierra realized that she had been holding tight to her childhood dreams, the fairy tale that promised her Prince Charming and unconditional love and affection. But Damien had not been genuine.

Tierra was kicking herself for having given up so much of herself to a man who had proven time and time again that he didn't deserve her. Tierra had known early in their relationship that Damien wasn't much interested in committing himself to a relationship with any woman. But she'd been holding on to hope since she'd been fourteen years old that he might change and be a better man.

Her grandmother had often told her that you can't change a man, so there was no point in trying. You either accepted him with all of his shortcomings or you moved on. Tierra had tried to accept Damien, but doing so had broken her spirit more times than she cared to count.

Tierra had gotten caught up in the illusion. She'd

dreamt of a perfect relationship and had gotten caught in the fantasy of what that was supposed to be. Daydreaming hadn't done her an ounce of good. But reality was proving to be a true guardian. Thoughts of Travis suddenly ran through her heart.

Tierra liked what she felt with Travis. Travis left her smiling from the inside out. The man made her giddy, and just thinking about him left her feeling like everything was right with the world. Even in her sadness, believing that her broken engagement was the end of her world, Travis had left her feeling on top of the world.

Their extended weekend had brought her joy like she'd not known before. Even in the short span of time they'd shared together, Tierra had known, beyond any doubt, that he was the man she wanted to spend the rest of her life with. She wanted to wash his dirty clothes and have dinner ready on his kitchen table when he came home from work at night. She wanted to have Travis Stallion's babies and raise his children to be as kind and as loving as their father. Travis was the man she wanted to sit on the front porch with when they were both old and gray, holding his arthritic hand in her own. Tierra smiled at the thought.

As the taxi pulled into the circular driveway, Tierra took a deep breath and then a second breath and a third. Her nerves were frazzled, anxiety tightening knots in the pit of her stomach. Travis had to know how much she wanted him. No matter what it took, she was determined to convince the man of her love.

Moving into the home, Tierra headed straight for

the kitchen and family room. Eden stood in the kitchen flipping through a stack of monthly magazines. The woman looked up, surprised to see Tierra alone.

"Hey, girl, when did you get back?"

"A few hours ago. Have you seen Travis?"

Eden shook her head. "Didn't you two come back together?"

Tierra heaved a deep sigh. "Eden, everything is such a mess! Damien was at my apartment when we got back."

Her best friend groaned, pushing her magazines from in front of her. "Say it's not so, Tea!"

"Mama Dee and Tingin found him waiting for me. He was still there when Travis and I got back."

"I really hope you threw his butt out, Tea!"

"I did, but Travis saw us kissing and left before I could explain anything."

"Why were you kissing Damien?"

"I wasn't. He kissed me and I slapped his face. Popped him good, but Travis didn't see me do that."

Eden shook her head. "They never do. Hold on," the woman said, reaching for a walkie-talkie sitting on the countertop. A minute later she smiled widely. "The housekeeper says Travis is in his room. She said he came in and went right upstairs."

Tierra twisted her hands together, her mind racing. "I need to go talk to him. But first..." She paused, her eyes skating from side to side. "Will you help me, Eden?"

"Tierra, you know you don't even need to ask. What's up?"

Tierra grinned. "Is there anything left over from breakfast?"

* * *

Travis imagined that he smelled burnt bacon. He sniffed the air, the aroma of overcooked pork filling his nostrils. He couldn't begin to imagine what someone was cooking downstairs, the breakfast hour long gone.

The unexpected knock on the door pulled him up off his bed. He couldn't imagine who in the family had gotten news of his return, but he still wasn't ready to be bothered with their queries about his trip or his time with Tierra. He was tempted not to answer at all, just wanting to revel in the pity party he was throwing for himself. The knock came again, more persistent the second and third time.

Crossing to the other side of the room, Travis pulled the entry open. Surprise registered across his face. Tierra stood on the other side of the door, a tray of badly cooked breakfast foods in her hand. Travis met her nervous gaze, a wide grin spanning his face as recognition set in.

"Okay, so I know it's not breakfast time, but I figured what the heck," Tierra said, pushing her way inside. "You and I always seem to do breakfast so well." She placed the tray onto the dresser, turning around to face the man.

Travis stood still holding onto the doorknob. He took a quick glance out into the hallway to see if she were alone, then finally closed the door, secreting the two of them away from any prying eyes.

Moving to her side, he stared down at the mess spread across the china plates. He looked from the food to Tierra and back again. "Did you cook this all by yourself?"

Tierra shrugged her thin shoulders skyward. "It had its challenges."

"What's that?" Travis asked, pointing to the lemon-colored mush that puddled in the center of a plate.

"Buttered grits."

Travis chuckled. "So, am I to understand that cooking isn't one of your strong points?"

"I am much better at takeout!" Tierra answered with a warm smile.

He shook his head and laughed.

Tierra moved to the bedside, dropping down against the mattress. As the two continued to eye each other, a pregnant pause filled the space between them.

"So..." Tierra finally said.

"So..." Travis responded.

An air of awkwardness rose like morning mist.

"Okay, so I did not kiss Damien. He kissed me, but I did not kiss him back. It really wasn't what it looked like. And I'm sure it looked like a lot."

Travis nodded. "Okay." He didn't sound convinced.

"And I'm *not,* I repeat, *not* interested in reconciling with Damien. I also made it clear to Damien that there was nothing else between us."

The man's head continued to nod.

"And I'm really mad at you!" Tierra's expression was animated, her hands flailing excitedly at her proclamation.

His eyebrows rose questioningly. "What are you mad at me for?"

"You left. You assumed the worse and you left. I thought you loved me!"

"I do love you, Tierra. More than you realize."

"Then promise me that you won't ever leave me like that again. I didn't appreciate that."

The man's smile was consuming. "Tierra, I had to give you some space. I know that—"

Tierra cut him off, shaking her head vehemently as she pointed a finger at him. "No, you were pouting, Travis Stallion. You thought I was going to give Damien a second chance, and so you had assumed the worst."

The man sighed as he moved to the bed and sat down beside her. "I wanted to give you a second chance, if that was what you wanted for yourself." Travis grabbed her hands, clasping them to his chest. "Tierra, I would understand if you really don't feel anything for me. I know that all of this has happened very fast. But more than anything, I want you happy. And if Private Porter makes you happy, then I would gladly back off and get out of his way."

Her smile was illuminating. "I would much prefer you claim me, Mr. Stallion. I can't be a good wife to you if you aren't willing to claim me."

Travis chuckled softly. "Yes, ma'am. Do you want to be my wife, Tierra? Because I am still very serious about us being together."

Tierra kissed his palm, pressing it to her cheek. "I have never, in my entire life, felt more loved than when I'm with you, Travis. I would do anything to make sure I never lost that."

Tierra and Travis savored the moment, trading easy caresses. They allowed the silence to swell fully around them. Outside, the sun was shining brightly.

"So," Travis said finally. "What now?"

Tierra pressed a manicured hand to his chest, drawing

it slowly down his abdomen until she reached the waistband of his slacks. "Why don't we get you out of these," she whispered, her sultry tone sending a shiver of energy down the man's spine. "They're in the way of something I want."

Travis sucked in air. "And what might that be?" he asked as Tierra unbuckled his belt.

Tierra's voice dropped to a loud whisper. "It'll be easier if I just show you," she said as she dipped her hand into the front of his pants and pulled down his zipper.

Travis was suddenly craving her touch. The wanting was intense, desire surging thick and full. He suddenly felt starved, desperate to be nourished by the nearness of her. He wrapped his arms around her torso, pulling her on top of him as he fell back against the mattress top. His mouth met hers in a frenzied kiss, the two of them consumed by the sweet ache that had taken control of their spirits.

Pulling at her clothes, Travis was gifted with her beautiful body. Inch after inch of caramel flesh became exposed, teasing him into submission. He was distracted by her breasts, the small pillows begging to be fondled. Grasping both in his hands, Travis leaned to suckle one and then the other. He slowly traced his tongue over her hardened nipples. He felt her shiver against him as he took her into his mouth, gently biting down against her flesh. Tierra inhaled swiftly, pleasure sweeping through her bloodstream.

She whispered his name, the lull of it sweet to his ears. In that moment, with the lilt of her tone caressing him from head to toe, he knew beyond any doubt that

Tierra loved him with everything in her. He also knew that he loved her even more.

Tierra placed her lips against his, the deep kiss arousing every nerve ending through his body. Aching for more, she inched her tongue into his mouth, sliding it along his tongue. Travis caressed her neck as they kissed, then let his hands glide the length of her back and sides.

Travis felt her slip her small hands between their bodies, her fingers kneading his abdomen and sliding across his chest. She pressed her pelvis against his, her hips slowly grinding into him. Travis groaned, arching his body up against hers. The length of his erection was solid steel as he pushed himself against her, eager to feel her body wrapped around his.

"I want to be inside you," Travis whispered into her ear, his deep vibrato pained with lust. "I want to feel you."

Kissing him again, Tierra hummed her consent into the man's mouth. Travis gestured to the nightstand and the box of condoms that rested there. Tierra pulled one from the container and ripped it open.

As she stretched the condom over his appendage, she stroked the length of him up and down between her palms. Travis groaned with rapture as the woman climbed above him and straddled his body. Lifting himself into her, Travis was awed by the sensation of Tierra's body locked around him, her inner lining clamping down hard against him.

As Tierra rode him, sliding him in and out of herself, she looked down into his eyes, her gaze locking with his. He clutched her hungrily, his hands gripping her buttocks as he pulled and pushed her against himself. Desire rushed like a storm wind between them, tears misting in both their eyes.

"You are so beautiful," Travis murmured, his stare sweeping across her face. He hugged her tightly, crushing her chest to his as he kissed her again and again, his tongue and lips dancing across her skin.

The moment was frenzied as Tierra's pace quickened, the reverie of the moment magnified tenfold.

Air caught in the young woman's chest as her breathing intensified. She was panting with want, perspiration beading against her skin. "I love you. God, how I love you!" Tierra cried, an orgasm ripping through her body.

And as Travis exploded with her, he screamed out the same, telling Tierra once again just how much he loved her.

Chapter 18

Tierra could only imagine what the Stallion family had to be thinking about the two of them. She and Travis had been closed up behind his locked door for two whole days, the staff leaving their meals on a tray outside the room.

It was either Matthew or John who'd knocked to make sure things were well, and once Travis had assured his family that they had nothing to be concerned about, everyone else had just left them alone.

They had been talking nonstop, ever since Tierra had delivered him that uneatable midday breakfast. Talking, making love and just enjoying the comfort of holding each other close. There was so much about each other that they didn't know, and the couple was trying to pack as much into the short time they had together as they could muster. Both were acutely aware that Travis didn't have much more time before he had to leave.

Tierra rolled her body against him, pressing herself along the line of his back as he slumbered peacefully. His body temperature was warm, inciting a wave of heat straight through her. Wrapping her arms around his torso, she pressed a damp kiss to the center of his back. The man felt so good in her arms.

Travis woke up in the middle of the night, a black sky peeking past the room curtains. Not even a partial moon shimmered in the dark. Tierra was wide awake, cuddled down in his arms, marveling at how much being in his arms felt like summer sunshine, banana pudding, a warm bubble bath and everything else she loved so much. Being in Travis's arms felt everything like home to her.

"Why aren't you asleep?" Travis murmured into her neck, kissing the soft flesh right behind her ear.

Tierra wiggled her backside against him. "Too much on my mind," she answered.

The man nodded his head against her.

"What's your favorite color?" Tierra asked.

"Red."

"Your favorite food?"

"Chicken, fried. And any kind of potato."

"Do you like animals?"

"Most. I'm not partial to anything too exotic. Iguanas and sheep don't give me any warm-and-fuzzy feelings."

Tierra laughed. "Iguanas and sheep?"

Travis shrugged his shoulders.

"Do you want children, Travis?"

"I'd love to have a child."

"Me, too. I definitely want kids. At least two."

"We will have as many as you want."

"Have you thought about living anyplace other than Texas?"

"I would consider living anyplace that benefited us and our family."

"Do soldiers make a good living? I mean, are you able to take care of a wife and family?"

Travis leaned up on his elbow, his head resting against the palm of his hand. "I make a very comfortable salary, and since I haven't had a whole lot of living expenses, the bulk of it has been invested or banked toward my savings. Suffice it to say, though, following my cousin John's advice has served me well, and I have quite a substantial portfolio and more than enough cash in the bank to live quite comfortably. I own a substantial amount of real estate, and truth be told, I'm what some might consider independently wealthy. You'll be able to have your house, the picket fence, two point four kids and a dog, in any state across the nation and most European countries, if that is what you want. If nothing else, Tierra, you can trust that you will want for absolutely nothing, and all you have to do is ask for everything you can possibly wish for."

Tierra giggled. "Whoa, I might like that." She paused, collecting her thoughts. "So, why do you stay in the military?"

"Because I love it. It gives my life a purpose. It honors everything I trust and value. I never imagined myself doing anything else. Why do you teach?"

Understanding blanketed Tierra's face. "It's what I was meant to do."

Travis pressed a damp kiss to her cheek. "So, what about you? What do you bring to the table, Ms. Braddy?

Because you are hardly a woman who needs or wants a man to take care of her."

Tierra smiled. "You're right. I don't need a man. I'm not as wealthy as you by any means, but I do very well for myself. I am tenured, so there is job security, and like you, I've invested my money well over the last few years. I own my home and also share a vested interest in my grandmother's property with my brother, should anything ever happen to her. My grandfather also left my brother and me a nice little nest egg when he passed."

Travis nodded. "You'll always have happiness and security with me. I believe in working hard, but I like to play hard, as well. I'd like us to kanoodle on the French Riviera while we sip expensive champagne!"

Tierra laughed with him. "I like how you think."

Travis lay back against the bed, curling his body around hers. Tierra grew quiet, falling back into reflection. Travis tightened the grip he had around her, hugging her close. Minutes later both fell back into a deep sleep.

An hour later, Tierra couldn't help but ponder what she might have done to have gotten so lucky. Damien walking out of her life had opened a door to happiness like Tierra had never known. She felt overwhelmingly blessed.

She pressed a warm palm to Travis's chest, her pelvis cradled against his buttocks. She smiled as Travis gripped her hand, threading his fingers through hers. She felt blessed beyond reason.

His body was still curled tightly against hers when Tierra rolled atop the mattress, turning to press her face against his broad chest. She inhaled deeply, savoring the scent of him, the warm mix of spice and evergreen teasing her nostrils. She pulled her hands to his chest, pressing the palms against Travis's bare skin. He smiled in his sleep, heaving a deep breath as she placed a kiss just beneath his chin, her tongue brushing a fine line across his Adam's apple. He stretched the length of his arms around her torso, pulling her to him, the protective gesture comforting.

Hours later as Travis leaned to kiss her forehead, then her closed eyelids, his lips strolling slowly until they reached hers, he shook the last fringe of sleep from his system, waking himself up fully. Outside, the sun had risen in a deep blue sky, searching for a corner of the universe to settle down in. A cooling breeze eased through the half-opened window, billowing the sheer curtains from side to side.

As Tierra dozed, Travis was determined not to disturb her. He snuggled down closer, her arms still wrapped tight around his chest.

The two had been talking about everything and absolutely nothing. Their conversations had gone from serious to silly and back again. Travis smiled. At one point they'd been discussing the nuances of lingerie and Tierra had taught him a thing or two about underwear. The lesson had been most enjoyable with Tierra's hands-on approach.

Tierra had burst out laughing when Travis had asked her what boy shorts were and why a woman would want to wear them. Slipping out of the linen slacks she wore, she'd rubbed her palms slowly along her hips, pointing out how nicely the cut of her pale pink panties flattered her feminine form. With perfect form, Tierra had noted how her very brief square-cut briefs had no front fly, designed specifically for a woman. Then she'd turned around, wiggling her butt cheeks to show how the silky fabric hugged her curves. The effect had been so sexy that Travis had almost come in his pants and Tierra hadn't even removed all her clothes.

Still in learning mode, Travis had been all too happy to complete the homework she then assigned him. He had stroked the fabric against her hips, then had teased her with the tip of his index finger. Tierra had purred with pleasure, closing her legs tight around his hand, as she rolled her hips sensuously against the bed.

It had given him great pleasure to pull Tierra's boy shorts off her bottom with his teeth. She'd rolled onto her stomach as he'd revealed her caramel bottom in all its lewd glory. Travis had teased her up and down with a gentle finger, enjoying the sight of her twin cheeks wriggling with delight.

When she'd rolled back around, sprawling her legs open, Travis could barely contain himself. He'd stripped quickly out of his clothes, sheathing his erection with a condom as it bounced against the mattress top. Grabbing Tierra's ankles for support, he'd slid into her with ease, the two sliding into place and locking themselves in a slow, mutual grind. Finding their rhythm, they'd rocked back and forth against each other. His breathing had quickened and Tierra had begged him not to stop. Her plea had almost been a whisper, but she had repeated it over and over again, the urgency for release consuming her.

With his mind and groin at the point of boiling

over, Travis had driven himself into her until they'd both dissolved into an erotic scream, Tierra shuddering around him.

Reflecting back, the memory shot a current of electricity straight through him. He palmed his crotch thinking about it, pleasure still consuming his spirit. As Tierra continued to sleep peacefully, Travis couldn't help but ponder what she might teach him about a thong.

John tilted his head in greeting as the couple made their way into the large family room. The rest of the family had already headed out for the day, everyone disappearing in different directions.

"Good morning," Tierra say cheerfully.

"Hey, cousin!" Travis exclaimed.

John smiled, a wide grin filling his face. "Glad to see you two come up for air. I thought we were going to have to send up a search party to rescue you both."

Tierra blushed, color flooding her warm complexion.

Travis laughed as they took a seat at the table. "Glad to see you still have a sense of humor, family."

John chuckled. "I'm sure you are. So, now that you two have come out of your dungeon, what's on your agenda today? Anything special planned?"

Travis nodded. "I'm glad you asked, John. I've had something on my mind and was hoping you might be able to give a brother a hand." He cut his eye toward Tierra, then returned his gaze to John.

Nodding, John sat forward in his seat. Tierra was suddenly curious, having no clue what Travis was referring to. John couldn't help but see her inquisitive stare.

Coming to his feet, John gestured with his head. "Why don't we take this to my office," he said casually. "Tierra, there's a fresh pot of coffee on the stove, and I'm sure you won't have any problems finding something to eat. Let me go see if I can solve your man's personal problem for him. I promise I'll bring him right back."

Winking in her direction, Travis followed his cousin out of the room. Bewildered, Tierra could only nod her head and wait. She rose from her seat, moving to the counter to get a ceramic cup and the pot of coffee. A plate of fresh-baked pastry beckoned for her attention. As she was prepping a plate of fresh fruit to accompany her pecan biscuit, Travis poked his head back into the room.

"Hey, sweet cheeks, you do have a passport, don't you?"

"Yes," Tierra answered, the curiosity filling her tone. "Why?"

Travis smirked, winked again and disappeared out of the room, not bothering to answer her question.

"I swear that man is trying to work my last nerve," Tierra said out loud, not expecting anyone to hear her.

From the doorway, Marah and Eden both burst out laughing.

"Sounds like you and Travis are getting along just fine," Eden said as they moved into the room.

Tierra laughed. "Where did you two come from?"

Marah grinned. "John said we were needed. What's going on?"

Shrugging, Tierra looked from one to the other. "Apparently you two know more than I do."

"And they don't know anything," John said as he stepped into the room behind them. "Not yet, anyway."

Travis was following close on his cousin's heels, a smug grin plastered across his face.

"Now I'm really curious," Tierra said, moving to her man's side. She wrapped her arms around his waist. "What's going on?"

Travis met his cousin's stare before smiling down at her. "It's a surprise," he said finally. "But we have to get a move on it."

"What… Where are we—" Tierra stammered as Travis pulled her along by the hand.

Travis gave a goodbye wave to everyone in the room. "I'll tell you on the way," he said.

Tierra shook her head, turning to wave goodbye, as well. Behind her, the Stallion clan beamed with joy, everyone waving at them excitedly.

I could really get used to this, Tierra thought as she settled back into the luxury accommodations, her palms caressing the leather on the armrests of their chairs.

Travis smiled down at her. "You should get used to this," he said, reading her mind. "I don't roll like this on a daily basis, but whenever you want we'll always go first class. Of course, I'm also very comfortable driving my Mustang, communing out of an apartment and eating home-cooked dinners three or four times a week. If you marry me I promise you'll have whatever lifestyle makes you comfortable. It can be as casual as you want, or not."

Tierra laughed. "Sergeant Stallion, you could move me into a tent in the middle of a desert and I would be perfectly content as long as I am with you. Just don't, though, 'cause you know I'm not good at camping."

Travis rolled his head, laughing with her. He leaned to kiss her cheek. "Baby, I promised you the world. You will definitely get that and whatever else I can muster up."

Leaning into his shoulder, Tierra settled down against him, resting her head on his arm. They'd been moving nonstop for the last three hours. Travis had thrown a few changes of clothing into an overnight bag and then they'd driven to her house for her to do the same thing. After checking that they both had their passports, they'd made a quick pit stop at the drugstore to pick up a few toiletries. From there they'd stopped by her grandmother's home to let the woman know they were both alive and well, Tierra having ignored her calls for the past two days. After a lengthy reprimand, Mama Dee had sent them on their way, and shortly after noon they were back at the airstrip boarding the Stallion jet for Mexico.

Marah, Eden and Marla were taking notes as John dictated Travis's wants. The three women were grinning from ear to ear, their excitement building exponentially.

"This just has to be incredible!" Eden exclaimed excitedly.

"Better than incredible," Marah concurred.

"I can't believe how fast it happened," Marla interjected. "Because it has happened really fast."

"I've never seen Travis so happy," John concluded. "He's floating right now."

Marah smiled. "Do you think they're making a mistake? I mean, maybe they should wait."

John shrugged ever so slightly. "You know, we've seen couples who've known each other for years marry, and the marriage fails. Do you remember meeting the Hale family at the company Christmas party?"

Marah nodded. "Yes, that couple with the twins, right?"

"Yeah, well, his parents lived together for some forty years without getting married. Happy as can be. Then they decided they needed to make it legal. They got married and six months later were separated and filing for divorce.

"You just never know. Travis and Tierra will probably be the type to get married and live happily ever after. I just think that if it's going to make them happy then they should give it all they've got."

The sisters all nodded in agreement.

"Well, I've got catering covered," Eden said. "And I'm headed out right now to order the cake."

"I called Tierra's brother, and he's going to let me into her apartment to get her wedding gown," Marla said. "I also spoke to Mama Dee, and she's on board."

"Reverend Patrick is available, but they have to get a license, and the state of Texas requires a seventy-two-hour waiting period after the license is issued. Has Travis even thought about the license?" Marah questioned.

John nodded. "Matthew is taking care of everything.

That new judge friend of his has pulled some strings or something. Since Travis is active military, they'll waive the seventy-two hours."

"Anything else?" Eden asked, looking at everyone around the room.

"The only other thing Travis asked for is that we try and get his friend Ross Knight here. Ross is a photographer out of Atlanta, and Travis wants him to do their wedding photos."

"We have some great photographers here in Dallas, if that's going to be a problem," Marah said. "I know a few of them."

John shook his head. "Travis wants Ross Oscar Knight, and only Ross. We'll give the man whatever he wants to get him here. Travis gave me a blank check and said that we are to spare no expense."

Marah smiled. "Now, if that doesn't sound like a Stallion man, I don't know what does."

Her husband chuckled. "That's how we do things, baby."

"Then I think that takes care of everything," Marla said with a wide smile. "All we need are the lovebirds."

Hugging his wife tightly, John pressed a kiss to her forehead. "They get back Wednesday, the day after tomorrow. Once they're here, we're having us a wedding!"

Chapter 19

The Cieba del Mar Beach and Spa Resort was minutes away from Cancún in Puerto Morelos. Stepping into the ocean-view room, Tierra and Travis were situated just minutes from their own private beach. The elegantly appointed suite was a laid-back, luxurious environment designed specifically for rest and relaxation, with its king-size bed, sitting area, terrace and private plunge pool.

"How long are we here for?" Tierra asked, clasping her hand in his.

Travis smiled. "Just a day or two. We have a commitment on Wednesday, and then I have to leave on Friday."

Tierra wrapped her arms around him and hugged him tightly. She was thrilled to be spending time with the man in such a beautiful place, but being reminded that it could only last but so long before Travis would be leaving her washed a wave of sadness through her spirit.

"So, what do you want to do first?" Travis asked, moving to open the patio doors.

Tierra followed behind him, dropping down onto one of the cushioned lounge chairs. She threw her hands up excitedly. "Absolutely nothing!"

Tierra lay in Travis's arms, her head resting comfortably on his chest. A warm breeze billowed through the room, the oceanic wind light and teasing. Outside, the sun was shining brilliantly, shimmering light on the airy white sand and the deep blue of the ocean water.

The couple had been resting comfortably from their morning excursions. They'd started the day with a couple's massage—an hour of having their muscles kneaded was pure euphoria—then a cocoon body wrap, scalp treatment and face massage. A short jaunt into Cancún to sightsee had left them spent by the time the midday heat had risen to full strength. Right after lunch they'd taken a slow stroll through the beautiful mangroves down to the meditation pier, where the birds serenaded guests through the afternoon.

Returning to the room, both were in need of a nap to prepare themselves for the dazzling experience the hotel staff had talked them into taking later that night. The Temazcal was an indigenous, ancestral ritual created to purify and renew their minds, bodies and spirits. It was performed at sunset, on the beach within a terra-cotta sweat lodge using hot volcanic stones and an infusion of aromatic herbs to obtain the steam. Travis imagined he needed much rest to prepare for steam and rituals.

He slowly caressed Tierra's shoulders and back, tickling the soft flesh beneath her clothes. The sensation was causing a ripple through her body, warmth settling comfortably within her. The last few days had bonded the two even closer together. He marveled at how much he'd come to know about the woman and, even more important, how much he wanted to know.

Tierra had opened herself to him, permitting him to witness those moments when she was most vulnerable, and he'd been moved by her passion for life and her sincere, loving spirit. He marveled at her energy and was inspired by her compassion. And what moved him most was feeling completely and totally confident that he had found his soul mate.

He hugged her closer, Tierra wrapping her leg around his, her body cradled against him. Leaning to kiss her forehead, Travis trailed a line of damp kisses along her profile, resting his mouth atop her mouth. His kiss was probing, his tongue snaking past the line of her lips to seek out hers. Dancing in hers, he was suddenly consumed with desire. Cupping the back of her neck, his thumb caressed her just under her ear. He felt her pulse jump, a smile widening across her face.

"You're trying to start something, Sergeant Stallion," she said, her demure tone teasing.

Travis continued to trail his hands across her flesh. "Yes, baby, I am." He kissed her hungrily. "I can't get enough of you, Tierra. Every time I touch you, I want more and more of you," he whispered huskily.

Returning his fervor, Tierra could only nod her head, understanding seeping through her. He hugged her tightly, his arms surrounding her in a gesture of comfort and protection.

Every time they made love, it was a thing of beauty. Their movements were fluid and natural, their instincts in perfect sync. Tierra marveled at the strength of his touch, his fingers inciting her nerve endings to explode with pleasure. Travis couldn't imagine the woman's kisses being more passionate. Each time he kissed her rivaled that first time he found himself kissing her. He couldn't begin to imagine anything sweeter.

His hand moved over her cheek, the soft skin teasing the pads of his fingers. When Tierra smiled, meeting his gaze evenly, he felt as if his heart might break with love. Her dark eyes shimmered in the light and he kissed her again. Wallowing in the embrace, Travis allowed her to take over the kiss, skin moving against skin, her lips and tongue moving with intensity as Tierra sucked and licked and tasted the sweetness of him. Her body arched and ached for more of his touch.

Travis moved his fingers across her forehead, brushing the strands of hair that had fallen in front of her eyes. He wanted to see her eyes as he brushed his lips over her checks and nuzzled the curve beneath her chin. He was awed by her beauty, consumed by the magnitude of her spirit and energy. A tear teased the corners of his eyes and he closed them tightly, fighting back the emotion. Closing his lids tightly, Travis inhaled the scent of her. The aroma of her perfume teased him, shivers quivering up his spine.

Lying beneath him, the crinkle of a smile pulled at Tierra's mouth. The man's touch was consuming, moving her to places and heights she didn't know possible. She gasped for air as Travis's hands moved to unbutton the buttons on her shirt. His touch was silk as his fingers skated along the line of her lace bra. Reaching behind her, Travis unclasped her bra and her breath quickened with anticipation. The sudden release of her breasts was overshadowed by his palms cupping them, heat coursing from his fingers straight into her heart. He tweaked her nipples until they hardened and Tierra bit down against her bottom lip at the sensation.

The sound of his belt being unbuckled and the zipper being pulled excited her. Travis's hands moved back to her body, gliding across her stomach to that sweet spot between her legs, taunting the swollen nub. His breath was heated against her, his lips following where his hands had led. Tierra moaned, pleasure sweeping through the room.

Their loving was bliss. Neither could begin to imagine that their intimate act would feel like the first time each time they were together. As Tierra clung to him hungrily, holding on for dear life, she knew that nothing and no one could ever move Travis Stallion from her heart.

After a wonderful meal of Caribbean shrimp and sweet potatoes in a spicy coconut sauce, the two had sat before an open fireplace, sipping on glasses of warm sherry, enjoying the ocean air. Travis had suggested they take a walk before retiring for the night.

A full moon sat high in the darkened midnight sky. Tierra and Travis strolled along the beachfront, hand in hand, the cool waves washing over their bare feet. In the distance lights flickered with a soft intensity, beckoning them forward.

"We have to leave tomorrow," Travis said softly, breaking the silence that had settled around them. "Then I'm back to Afghanistan."

Tierra nodded. "I don't want you to go."

"I don't want to go, either, but I have to."

Tierra squeezed his hand, her other palm lightly caressing his arm. "If I haven't told you already, Travis, I want you to know how much the last few weeks have meant to me. Even with all that drama with my ex, I would do it all over again if I had to."

Travis stopped, turning to face her. He clasped her face between his palms, staring deep into her eyes. "Tierra, I love you. And I think you know how much I love you. So…" Travis dropped down to one knee. Reaching into his jacket pocket he pulled a small velvet box into his hand, flipping it open to expose a stunning emerald-cut diamond ring in a lavish platinum setting.

He pulled Tierra's left hand into his own, staring up into her eyes as he continued. "At this moment, I am kneeling before you with my heart in my palms, offering it to you, Tierra Braddy. I love you. I want to spend my life with you. I need you by my side as I leap into the future. I want you to be my wife. Will you marry me?"

Tierra gasped, the moment surreal. She dropped to her knees beside him, her mouth meeting his in a divine kiss. "I do love you, Travis. I didn't know it was possible to feel what I'm feeling for anyone. But you have it like no one has ever had my heart before. Yes. Yes. I would be honored to be your wife."

Travis's grin was a mile wide as he slipped the ring onto Tierra's ring finger and placed a kiss into the palm of her hand. He wrapped his arms around her, drawing her into a deep embrace. He kissed her excitedly, joy filling his spirit as it danced in sync with hers.

They'd talked and walked the length of the beach for hours. Out of nowhere a sudden rain storm showered down from the sky. The downpour was heavy, the kind of rain that soaks deep into a body within minutes. Neither of them seemed to notice as they kicked their way through the sand, still holding hands. The sky had grown even darker, so much so that Travis could barely see Tierra standing beside him. A flash of lighting suddenly illuminated her exquisite face.

Enamored, Travis pulled Tierra to him, kissing her deeply as rain ran like a river over their heads. Tierra kissed him back, her tongue pushing eagerly past his lips into his mouth to dance alongside his own. Bolstered by her enthusiasm, Travis slid his hand beneath her skirt, her clothing saturated through to her panties. Tierra moaned her excitement into his mouth as he slid his fingers beneath the fabric, pressing his thumb over the hardened nub between her legs. As he drew slow circles against her flesh, making her draw her breath through her teeth, Tierra slid her leg up his, her knee resting against his hip.

Moving his mouth to her neck, Travis nuzzled the soft flesh, his tongue teasing the lobe of one ear and trailing the line of her chin to the other lobe. Tierra popped the buttons to his shirt, her hands moving across his broad chest.

With his hand still dancing against her secret garden, Travis kissed her again, their connection so sweet that

Tierra couldn't imagine anyone moving her spirit the way he did. No one before him had ever kissed her like Travis kissed her. Travis's lips ignited fires deep in her belly, shooting fireworks through every nerve ending and turning her knees to jelly. If it were not for his strong arms encircling her waist or her arms latched around his neck, she'd have melted to the ground. Instead, she strained against him, needing him fiercely, longing to be one with him. The feelings were so strong they scared her, yet she couldn't break free. She would have stopped breathing first.

She wanted to protest when he drew away. The cool evening air chapped her sore, swollen lips. Travis's gaze smoldered into hers. "Let's take this back to our room," he whispered. "It's too cold out here for you." His teeth nipped her earlobe, and then his tongue bathed her ear. Arching her neck, she shivered against him.

Lifting her into his arms, Travis leaned his head back, his raspy breathing mimicking hers. Tierra nuzzled her face into his neck, her arms draped around his shoulders. With the rain still falling around them, he carried her back across the beach to the patio outside their room. By the time he maneuvered them through the sliding-glass doors to lay her across the bed's comforter, Tierra was completely naked beneath him. Standing back to take in the view, he was totally enamored with the sight of her.

Travis wanted her badly, and he sensed that Tierra wanted him just as much. He rubbed the goose flesh of her cold skin as he admired her body. Tearing his wet clothes away from his own body, he stood completely naked. Leaning over her, he took her face into his hand, kissing her lips passionately. Her hands whispered across his skin, tracing the powerful muscles of his back.

Cupping her small breasts, he kissed them gently. Her nipples hardened beneath his touch as he ringed first one and then the other, teasing back and forth with his tongue. Tierra moaned expressively, unable to contain her excitement.

Moving her hands to grasp his manhood, she stroked him easily. When her ministrations became too much, Travis pushed her hands away and reached for a condom that rested atop the nightstand. As Tierra helped him with the prophylactic, he gasped for air. Rolling her back against the bed, Travis supported himself on his forearms and began to slowly pump his body back and forth. With each stroke he drove into her, crushing her soft breasts against his hard chest. Tierra whimpered faintly, urging him in with her hands.

As release claimed them, both sheened in sweat despite the chill in the air, the rain outside continued to dance down, tapping eagerly at the window.

Chapter 20

There were two limos waiting side by side when they stepped off the private jetliner onto the tarmac. Tierra's stare was questioning as she looked from Travis to the driver, who was beckoning for her attention.

"What's going on?" she asked curiously.

Travis gave her a breathtaking smile, his eyes glistening with joy. "We have to go get ready. I will see you later this afternoon," he answered as he leaned to kiss her cheek. He gave her a gentle push toward the car, the driver swinging the door open for her.

"Bye, and I love you," Travis said as he gave her a quick wink, moving toward the other vehicle.

Tierra was still standing there looking stunned when she heard her name being called from inside the car. Leaning to peer inside, she was greeted with smiles and laughter, Eden, Marah, Marla and her grandmother all waving excitedly.

"Girl, get in this car. We have a million things to do," Mama Dee chimed.

"What's going on?" Tierra asked, looking from one to the other.

Eden grabbed her left hand, holding it up in the sunlight.

"Nice!" Marah exclaimed. "Very nice!"

"That boy's got good taste," Mama Dee said, admiring Tierra's engagement ring.

The young woman beamed. "Isn't it gorgeous!"

"I'm just glad you said yes," her grandmother responded. "Now we've got to go get you ready."

Tierra eyes widened. "Ready for what?"

"Your wedding, of course. Travis said you would be his wife before he left to return to duty, and we promised to help make that happen."

Eden leaned forward in her seat. "You do want to marry him, right, Tierra?"

Four pairs of eyes focused intently on her face. Mama Dee's eyebrows were raised in query. They all stared as Tierra seemed to mull over the question, the answer coming to her slowly. Then she nodded, a deep smile filling her face.

"I do. I want to marry Travis Stallion more than anything else in this world."

Her grandmother laughed, the deep chortle filling the car's interior with glee. "That's my girl!"

Eden nodded her agreement. "Well, then, let's go get you ready for a wedding.

The next three hours were a complete blur. Manicures and pedicures were followed by a trip to the hair salon. When all of the women were primped and pampered, they returned to the ranch for a light lunch before it would be time to get themselves dressed for the wedding.

The women were joking and laughing, telling Tierra about their own nuptials and the extremes that had been taken to get their men down the aisle.

"Your granddaddy thought he was slick," Mama Dee said with a deep chuckle. "He thought he was going to get the milk without buying the cow. I had to set him straight real quick."

Tierra laughed. "Papa Jake loved you."

"Yes, he did, baby. Your granddaddy said I was the best thing that ever happened to him. And I was," Mama Dee said, her face beaming with glee.

The matriarch moved to Tierra's side. "I have to ask you this one more time," her grandmother said, as she reached to lower the flame on the teapot that was just beginning to simmer for attention. "You know you don't have to do this if you're not ready, right? You do want to marry this man, right?"

Tierra smiled, pausing as she stirred a teaspoon of sugar into the tall glass of lemonade. The kitchen was suddenly warmer than usual, and Tierra knew it had nothing to do with the heat wafting off the large black burners or coming from inside the oven, where a pan of quiche was just beginning to set. Since she'd first laid eyes on the man, every thought of him caused a rise in her temperature. She shook the sensation, taking a deep breath. "Yes," she answered, the surety in her tone undeniable.

Mama Dee leaned to kiss her granddaughter's cheek. "Just checkin'!" The older woman reached out a wrinkled hand and pressed her fingers to the spot where her lips had just grazed. "That man loves you, Tierra. I feel it with ever fiber in my body. And you love him, too. But that's not enough. You and Travis are going to have to grow into this relationship. There are still some things y'all don't know about each other, and you might discover some things y'all don't like about each other. But if you want it to work bad enough, you can make that happen. Just hold tight to the love and let it grow with you."

Nodding, Tierra leaned her head against her grandmother's chest as the woman wrapped her in a deep embrace. Both women wiped a tear from their eyes, trying not to burst out crying. "Girl, you're going to ruin my makeup," Mama Dee exclaimed warmly. "Now finish up your meal so you can go put that dress on and let us all see how pretty you're going to look going down that aisle!"

Travis was laughing warmly as his cousins made joke after joke about his impending nuptials. The men had gone for a quick lunch, each enjoying a cold beer before returning to the ranch to prepare themselves for his wedding.

As he stepped out of the limousine he was momentarily taken aback by the preparations that had already been attended to. A staff of dozens was scurrying around to ensure that the ceremony and reception went off without a hitch. The women had arrived back just minutes before them, and Eden and her sisters were giving orders with exact precision.

The oldest sister hurried to his side, a wide smile filling her face. "Hey there! Are you excited?"

Travis chuckled warmly. "And scared to death!" he said, his tone teasing.

Eden brushed a warm palm against his arm. "Everything is going to be perfect. Now—" she glanced down to the page of notes in her other hand "—the chapel is ready, so make sure you take a peek inside. If there is anything you need or want in there, just let me know."

"It's filled with roses, right?"

She nodded. "Every single one between here and the Mexican border."

Travis laughed.

"After the ceremony, Ross wants you and Tierra to go down to the pond for some photos."

Travis looked around excitedly. "Is he here?"

"Yes," Eden answered with a nod. "He's around here somewhere assessing the best lighting and angles and whatever else it was he said he needed to make sure the photos were perfect. We've assigned two assistants to take care of anything he needs. I'm sure he'll catch up with you soon."

"Great!"

"While you and Tierra are enjoying a few minutes of private husband-and-wife time getting your picture taken, your guests will be gathering for a cocktail reception on the front lawn. Then they'll be led into the barn for the reception.

"You're going to love the barn. The band is already setting up and the air-conditioning is on high, so it will be comfortable for the crowd."

"Can I take a peek inside there, too?" Travis questioned.

Eden nodded. "Of course. We're using long white linens, white plates on gold chargers, a ton of candles and we've even lit up the twig chandeliers. It will be absolutely gorgeous. Tierra is going to love it! We've got the perfect combination of charming, rustic and elegant."

Travis wrapped the woman in a warm embrace. "Thank you. I know everything is going to be great, and you don't know how much I appreciate it all."

Eden smiled. "I know that you have made one of my best friends the happiest woman in the world. None of us can ask for anything more."

Inside the chapel, arrangements of white roses decorated the altar and pews, the delightful fragrance wafting through the midday air. Whether she had admitted it or not, Tierra was definitely a rose kind of girl, and Travis was certain that she'd be completely delighted with his flower selections.

With his arms crossed over his chest, he didn't know where to focus his eyes first, in awe of the magnitude of it all. Mark and Matthew stepped up behind him, and Matthew dropped a large hand against his shoulder.

"So, you certain about this, big guy?"

Travis nodded. "More certain than I have ever been about anything. I love that woman."

Mark nodded. "I knew when Mitch and I were headed cross-country that I wanted to do the same thing. And we didn't wait. Stopped down in New Orleans and made it legal. And I don't regret one minute of it."

Matthew laughed. "He almost did when he got back and these women found out they couldn't plan his wedding. They like to throw a party now!"

The three chuckled warmly.

"Well, I'm glad I could get their help with mine," Travis said, looking from one to the other. He inhaled, air filling his nostrils with the floral scent.

"Travis," Reverend Joshua Patrick called out. "How are you, son?"

Travis smiled as he extended his hand in greeting, the three men acknowledging the minister who'd moved into the space beside them.

"Reverend Patrick, thank you for coming," Travis said with a warm smile. "I greatly appreciate this."

The man nodded. "Do you think we can sit down for a minute? I'd like to talk with you, Travis."

Matthew looked down to his wristwatch. "You gentlemen have at it. Travis, the men are getting dressed down at the conference center. When you're ready that's where you'll find your tuxedo waiting for you." He tapped his cousin's shoulder.

Nodding, Travis moved beside the minister, who'd taken a seat on the front pew.

"Marriage is a very serious commitment, son," the pastor started, forgoing the small talk. "Usually, I don't marry anyone until they've gone through pre-marital counseling with me."

Travis smiled. "I know, sir. And I appreciate your understanding our time constraints."

"I had a very nice chat with your young lady. She's very grounded in her faith. She's also got a good head on her shoulders. But I would be remiss if I didn't ask you both some serious questions to ensure that you're headed in the right direction."

"Yes, sir."

"Do you trust Tierra, Travis?"

"With everything I have, sir."

"What will you do if you cannot agree?"

Travis smiled. "Tierra is extremely strong-willed when she wants to be. I'm sure there will be much compromising, and on occasion, I may even have to concede to her best judgment as I would hope she would concede to mine, if need be. I do know though there will always be an open line of communication. I will keep talking to her and encouraging her to share her feelings with me."

The minister nodded. "With you headed back to Afghanistan, you two are starting your marriage off in a very unconventional manner. You're essentially committing your lives to each other today, and then tomorrow you'll be apart for the next twelve months or so. How will you continue to bond as a couple as well as build your relationship with so much distance between you?"

Travis paused, reflecting on the gravity of the question. He and Tierra had talked in great depth about what might happen once he returned to his duties. Neither could deny the seriousness of his situation.

"Reverend Patrick, Tierra has promised me her love and support, and I have pledged to give that back to her tenfold. I don't know what might happen to me once I report back to duty. I don't know if I'll survive tomorrow without being hit by a bus. I just know that right now, today, I love that woman with everything in me. I pray daily that God will wrap his hands around this union and support and nourish it.

"There won't be a day that goes by that I won't tell Tierra how much I love her and want the best for her. And I will share everything I have in me to share, with her and only her. I stand on the power of faith that she will do the same."

The two men continued talking, the minister throwing questions at Travis and Travis answering them from his heart. When John poked his head into the room to let them both know that Travis needed to get dressed if the ceremony was going to start on time, Reverend Patrick nodded.

Rising from his seat, he extended his hand in Travis's direction, the two shaking hands easily. "Son, I wish you and Tierra much success. I am honored to be able to bless this union this afternoon. I think you should go get yourself ready. You definitely don't want to keep that pretty lady waiting."

Travis grinned. "Thank you, sir. And no, I don't. I wouldn't want her to change her mind," he said teasingly.

His pastor laughed with him. "Son, I do not think you have anything to worry about!"

Chapter 21

Tierra had not known it possible to be so happy. Staring out to the swell of activity outside, she was mesmerized by the sheer magnitude of what was about to happen. The grounds had been transformed, and she couldn't wait to see what Travis had designed for their wedding ceremony. Knowing that he'd spent the last four weeks discovering what she'd wished for herself, she instinctively knew that she would not be disappointed.

Turning to admire her reflection in the full-length mirror, Tierra took a deep breath. The woman who stared back at her was confident and sexy, determined and beautiful. She had waited her whole life to be in this place with a man whose love for her was all encompassing. She passed her hands down the length of her dress, fanning the skirt of her gown around her small frame.

Her Monique Lhuillier gown had been donated

to a women's shelter to be auctioned at their annual fundraising event. This gown, a Manuel Mota original, had been flown in from Barcelona, Spain, specifically for her. The delicate, classical gown was layers of sumptuous embroidered lace and silk taffeta. Her wedding gown was everything she had ever hoped it would be, and Travis had made it all possible.

Tierra believed beyond any doubt that Travis loved her with all his heart. She knew that she loved him as much, if not more. She was excited at the prospect of their future, eager to see what fate had in store for them.

Understanding that they still had much to learn about each other, Tierra was excited by the possibilities. Every day forward would be a day of exploration and learning for them. Time would be a welcome friend as they grew together, determined to reach new heights hand in hand.

As Eden stood in the doorway telling her it was time for the ceremony, Tierra closed her eyes and whispered a prayer skyward, giving thanks for the blessings of that moment and for the man she was ready to promise herself to.

Travis walked the length of the cobblestoned courtyard back toward the chapel. Understanding that he needed just a few minutes to himself, his family had gone on ahead, awaiting his arrival for the ceremony. The late-afternoon air was exceptionally warm but comfortable. Taking a deep breath, Travis willed away the rise of anxiety that had nestled in the pit of his stomach. Nervous energy was abundant.

Had anyone told him that a chance meeting would have changed the entire direction of his life, he would not have believed them. He was completely in awe of everything that had changed for him since that day he'd stepped out of the elevator at Tierra's apartment and had seen her standing there in the hallway.

With much certainty, Travis knew that Tierra completed him. Tierra had been that one thing that he had been longing for even when he hadn't had a clue that anything was missing from his life. Tierra was that one piece that completed all of his puzzles.

He would never have imagined any woman having his heart so completely, but Tierra did. He had relinquished every ounce of himself to her, heart and soul. He loved that woman beyond reason, and he was excited by the prospect of them sharing the rest of their days with each other.

Pausing just outside the door of the chapel, Travis's only regret was that his parents couldn't be there to share this day with him. But as his cousin Mark gestured in his direction, waving him to stand with his family at the altar, his heart lifted with abundance. He had family who loved him immensely and family he loved just as much.

As he moved to the front of the church, clasping his hands in front of him, he looked out over the friends and family who had gathered to celebrate the occasion with them. The joyous energy filled the room, the magnificence of it almost overwhelming. Luke tapped him on the shoulder, his head nodding ever so slightly. Travis smiled at the four men by his side, the brothers of his soul who had helped make this moment possible. He had family, and it brought him the greatest joy to have Tierra want to be his family, as well.

Ever so thankful, Travis lifted his gaze, thoughts of praise being carried toward the clouds on a gust of breeze that seemed to rise just for that reason and blow warmly. He was thankful for their health, their spirits and the wealth of love between them. He was thankful, and he wanted everyone to know how much.

As if they'd transported the Stallion rose gardens into the chapel's interior, brilliant white roses adorned the altar and decorated the end of each pew. The sweet nectar scented the late-afternoon air, reminding Travis of the time in the gardens when he first realized that Tierra had hold of his heart. Tiered candles shimmered between the blooms, casting a warm glow around the space and Travis was excited for Tierra to walk into the room. He said a quick prayer that it would be everything she had ever imagined for herself.

Beside him, his four cousins stood regally in charcoal to gray tuxedos. Their pristine white shirts and black bow ties were accentuated by velvet red boutonnieres. Standing to the right side of the family minister, Marla, Eden and two of Tierra's cousins stood in silver-gray ball gowns, bouquets of red roses held primly in front of them. The women were smiling and dabbing away tears of excitement.

As a trio of flutists began to play the Wedding March, announcing the bride's arrival, Travis eagerly searched the back of the church. As Tierra stepped inside, her brother, Tingin, escorting her down the aisle, tears swelled full in his eyes.

The exquisite woman was angelic as she glided toward him, fighting to hold her own tears at bay. She had never looked more beautiful. Stepping to his side, her mouth lifted in smile, and Travis wanted nothing more than to taste the sweetness of her lips. As Tingin passed her hand into his hand, every ounce of nervousness wafted out the door.

A wide grin spread across the man's face. Tierra's excitement was consuming as he pressed his cheek to hers, whispering into her ear that he loved her. She grinned in response, her love shimmering like ice in her eyes.

Hand in hand the couple exchanged their wedding vows, both promising each other an eternity of love and devotion to one another. When Reverend Patrick pronounced them husband and wife, Mama Dee cheered loudly, clapping her hands as a "Praise Jesus" rang through the air.

With the happily married couple off for pictures, the Stallion family gathered together for a few minutes to admire their handiwork.

"It was a beautiful wedding!" Joanne Lake, Luke's fiancée, exclaimed. "And what an absolutely gorgeous bride!"

Everyone nodded their agreement.

"So, who's next?" Eden asked, looking from Matthew to Luke and back again.

"Yeah," Marla interjected, "we've gotten this wedding thing down to a science. Which one of you Stallion boys are we going to get to work our magic on next?"

Luke laughed as Joanne shook her head.

"We like being engaged," Joanne said sweetly. "We're in no rush, thank you very much."

Matthew held up both hands. "Do not look at me."

"No, we're looking at you," John interjected. "I'm hearing an awful lot of rumors about you, boy!"

"Ditto that!" Mark chimed as he caressed his wife's pregnant belly. "Baby rumors, female rumors, all kinds of rumors."

Matthew blushed. "Don't believe everything you hear."

"How is Vanessa, by the way?" Luke asked, inquiring about their very pregnant family friend.

Matthew smiled. "The last I heard, she was still pregnant."

"But is she still a lesbian?" Luke asked. "Inquiring minds want to know!"

"I want to know about your new judge friend," John teased. "The woman who helped with Travis's marriage license. Seems you two have been spotted together around town a lot lately. Something we should know about, little brother?"

Matthew laughed, the warmth of it flooding his dark face. "Why, John, I don't know what you're talking about."

Marla moved to John's side, wrapping her arms around her husband's waist. "Does the brother protest too much?" she said with a sly laugh, everyone laughing with her.

Matthew smirked, still shaking his head. "Y'all are some nosy people."

The group laughed.

Marah shook her head. "I think it's starting to get hot up in here!"

Nodding his agreement, Matthew headed in the direction of the bar. "Don't you know, sister dear, we wouldn't be true Stallions if we didn't bring some heat!"

Chapter 22

With their wedding guests still dancing the night away, Tierra and Travis politely said their goodbyes and disappeared to a lavishly appointed suite at the Hotel Palomar. The artful boutique accommodations couldn't have been more special. The rich, earth-toned color scheme was a wonderful backdrop for the wealth of roses that adorned the room. Only Travis knew just how much Tierra loved her roses.

Retiring into a jetted soaking tub, Tierra lay between Travis's legs, the water washing away the urgency that had consumed most of their day. With his arms wrapped tightly around her torso, her back cradled tight against his chest, Tierra couldn't remember having ever been happier.

"Thank you," she whispered softly, peering up to meet his gaze.

"For what?" Travis questioned, pressing a moist kiss to the top of her head.

"For the most perfect day any woman would ever wish for."

Travis smiled as he hugged her closer. "It was perfect because of you, Tierra. You don't know how happy you have made me."

A smiled pulled at Tierra's mouth, saline glistening in her eyes. She clasped her arms around his, cuddling down against him. The two lay together for some time just enjoying the quiet of each other's company. Tierra lavished beneath Travis's touch as he cupped his palm full of warm water and trickled it down the length of her arms and over her breasts and abdomen. The light, feathery strokes of his fingers sent trickles of electricity through her, her whole body tingling with pleasure.

"Why don't we take this into the bedroom," Tierra whispered, her seductive tone low and teasing. "I have something I want to show you."

Travis beamed. "I like the sound of that, Mrs. Stallion."

Rising from the tub, Tierra passed him a large, plush towel. "I'll be waiting," she said, moving away from him toward the other room.

Minutes later when Travis stepped inside, Tierra was splayed out across the bed top, a red bra and thong set adorning her petite frame. The man smiled broadly.

"Nice!" Travis exclaimed, his eyes widening with desire. "Very nice."

"Since you lost the receipt and I couldn't return it," Tierra said, her index finger trailing over the lace between her breasts, "I figured we needed to put it to good use."

"I like the way you think, baby!"

Tierra shifted up to her knees, beckoning him to her. As she did, an erection lengthened beneath the damp towel tied around Travis's waist, his member full and engorged. Travis let the towel drop to the floor at his feet as he moved himself toward his new wife. Just as he neared the bedside, Tierra gripped his hand with hers and pulled him to her.

Like a puppy on a leash, Travis followed willingly, dropping down onto the bed as Tierra rolled them over until she was lying sprawled on top of him. Her brilliant smile hinted at her intentions, sending a shiver of desire into Travis's groin. Blood surged, making him harder than he ever remembered being.

Using her knees, Tierra pushed his legs apart. Her small hands took full control of his body, traveling hungrily over his flesh as she claimed possession of his sex, and his mind. Reaching for her, his hands were slapped lightly away.

"Don't move, soldier," Tierra commanded, pushing him back against the mattress.

"Yes, ma'am," Travis whispered huskily, falling back against the bed.

Tierra's lips followed where her hands led. She trailed hot kisses across his neck and shoulders, sweeping over his chest, back down to his taut abdomen. The heated teasing was like fire and brimstone against his skin. Travis began to rock and grind against her, his wanting about to erupt with a vengeance.

Pushing down against him, Tierra teased him with

promises of what was still to come, her pelvis grinding against his. As his jagged breathing increased in tempo, Tierra continued her oral assault, stopping to dip her tongue into the curve of his belly button.

Travis cried out her name as Tierra took him into her mouth. Her sweet lips were wrapped around his manhood as her hot, serpent-like tongue slathered him with affection. It was almost too much for him to handle as he struggled not to explode, his whole body throbbing with anticipation.

"Not yet," Travis groaned softly.

Tierra suddenly felt him, his hands everywhere, pulling her against him as he flipped her over onto her back, pushing her back against the bed. He gripped the cheeks of her behind tightly, a wild, abandoned look of pure desire staring down at her.

"Don't make me come yet!"

Tierra pulled herself against the center of the bed as Travis knelt down between her thighs. Before she could inhale, she felt his tongue searching, and she marveled at the soft strokes he painted against her skin. The sensation was incredible as she pushed herself against his mouth, wanting more. Then, just as she felt her temperature rising, her pulse starting to race, the length of his body hovered above her and she gasped as the length of his manhood pushed against the door of her femininity and eased its way inside. Travis entered her easily, claiming what was rightfully his.

His strokes were slow at first, an easy tempo against the walls of her flesh. Sinking deeper and deeper into the fleshy folds, his pace quickened, the elongated strokes filling every niche and crevice until there was no more of him for her to take and no more of her left to fill.

His loving became fast and furious, his want of the woman controlling every move. Their orgasm was intense, coming in perfect unison. When Tierra screamed, pleasure sweeping through her body, he collapsed, the essence of her name rolling over his tongue. Lying with their bodies cradled tightly together, neither one of them wanted to imagine the moment when it would have to end.

Chapter 23

The young soldier announcing he had mail lifted Travis's spirits beyond reason. The last three months had truly taken a toll on his spirit, and knowing that he still had five more to go wasn't doing him much good. He couldn't begin to explain to anyone how much he missed his wife. Being so far from Tierra was beginning to wear him down.

The large box and bundle of letters were exactly what he needed. Exhausted, he couldn't begin to imagine anything lifting the funk that had settled down over them all. The night before had been particularly challenging. Sirens had blared as a Taliban rocket attack across the Kandahar Air Field sent them all spinning for the second time in a week. Units had moved into cement-reinforced bunkers waiting for an all-clear. The near-death experience had him and his platoon on high alert, and the anxiety was challenging.

Retreating into his quarters, Travis ripped open the first of what seemed like a dozen or more letters. The government seal on the first envelope indicated its seriousness, requiring his full and immediate attention. Short, sweet and to the point, Travis digested its contents, mulling the information over in his head before replacing it in its mailer.

He slid it beneath his pillow, making a mental note to share its details with Tierra the first opportunity he had. A smile pulled at his lips as he sat the other letters onto his lap.

Tierra had promised him she would write every day and every night, detailing how her day had gone. She'd been back to school for some time, and her letters kept him included on the little faces who spent time with her each and every morning. He laughed at the antics of her kindergarten class, and with each salutation, Tierra telling him she loved and missed him, his heart ached to get back home.

Two hours later Travis had read each letter twice, annoyed that mail took so long to reach him that it would be another week or more before the next stack of letters would take him back to Texas and the woman he loved, if only for a brief time.

Those first few weeks back had been the hardest. Travis had actually imagined himself throwing in the towel and going AWOL to ease the hurt of it all. Private Porter had thought to challenge him only once, but it hadn't taken much for Travis to convince him that he was not the man and this was not the place. Eventually, Private Porter had let go of his animosity, finding solace in the arms of a young woman far from his home.

Just weeks earlier, the soldier had been transferred to another platoon. Travis had shaken his hand and wished him well, both men moving forward on very different paths.

The large box beckoned for his attention. The Ross Oscar Knight Photography logo adorned the return address label. Travis's excitement increased substantially as he pulled out a pocket knife and flipped open the blade to slice the taped seam.

Reaching inside, he peeled back layers of protective tissue paper to expose the leather-bound wedding album. The commemorative book had been embossed with his and Tierra's names and the date of their wedding ceremony. A full grin spread like fire across Travis's face as he pulled it from the packing material, easing it onto his lap. He'd been anxiously awaiting this package since he and his good buddy Ross Knight had shaken hands goodbye, Ross boarding a jet to Italy to shoot another wedding. Travis hadn't been able to express what it had meant to him to have his friend share in such a special time in his life.

Lifting the cover, Travis beamed at the first picture of him and Tierra together. She'd been extraordinarily beautiful in that incredible dress that had meant so much to her. He'd been quite dashing himself in his dress blues, the military uniform honoring everything he believed in. They made a pretty couple, if he said so himself.

Turning each page one by one, Travis was even more enamored by the wealth of beauty before him. It was a thing of sheer joy manifested upon the pages, and Ross had managed to capture in images emotion that could barely be captured with words.

The visuals were overwhelmingly breathtaking, capturing the embodiment of colors and textures that had meant so much to Tierra. Ross had made the most simple aspects of their wedding ceremony look so darn pretty. Travis could only imagine how Tierra had reacted when her own photo album had arrived. What had translated to film couldn't be denied. It was truly a wonderful piece of photo-telling.

Glancing down to his wristwatch, Travis tucked his album beneath the pillow on his bed. Grabbing his equipment, he headed for the communications room and the computer and Web cam that enabled him to see Tierra once each month.

The time each soldier had was limited, and Travis imagined that it would take an act of God to keep him from his scheduled appointment. He knew that Tierra was already logged into her computer waiting for his connection, and he was determined not to disappoint her for their date night.

Sitting at the desk in her spare bedroom, Tierra turned on the laptop that rested there. As the unit powered on, Tierra moved to the room's large mirror to check her face and makeup. She wanted Travis to see her at her best.

She smiled, her reflection shimmering with the happiness that spilled from her eyes. All she wanted was for Travis to see her happy. Since his departure, she'd worried nonstop. She'd probably cried just as much. She hadn't thought it possible to miss a man as much as she found herself missing her man. Every morning she counted down the days to his return, anxious for the moment when he would set foot back on Dallas ground and back into her arms.

Their last days together had been the best days of Tierra's life. The quick excursion to Mexico had allowed them to relax in each other, the honeymoon before the honey. Hours after landing back in Dallas, Travis had stood before a congregation of their family and friends and had claimed her, just like he'd promised to do. They had pledged their love and loyalty to one another, the minister proclaiming them husband and wife. The moment had been witnessed by the people who loved them best, and Tierra couldn't have imagined a more perfect wedding.

She took a big inhale of breath as she moved back to her seat, logging onto her computer. Next to the laptop a framed photo of Travis smiled at her. It had been her favorite photo from the wedding, Travis's friend Ross capturing the one moment that had meant the world to her.

After meeting the man, Tierra had understood why having Ross capture their special day had meant so much to Travis. Ross had listened to their story, had felt the joy in their experience and had promised to deliver a portfolio that would leave them speechless. Ross had shared stories of his and Travis's friendship with her, and it had taken no time at all for Tierra to consider the man her friend, as well.

When Ross had asked her what she wanted most from their wedding photos, she knew that there was one single moment he could capture that would mean more to her than any other. Tierra had asked him to capture Travis's expression the first time he saw her in her gown, heading down the aisle in his direction.

Reaching for the framed photo, Tierra delighted in the sheer beauty of it. Each time she studied the image, she was in awe of the emotion that seeped out of Travis's eyes. Ross had captured every ounce of love the man had for her, and when she looked at the photograph what she saw in Travis's eyes had been manifested a hundred times over.

That moment encompassed what she felt most when Travis looked at her. The wealth of his gaze made her feel beautiful and exceptionally special, his stare warming her spirit like nothing else.

The computer beeping pulled at her attention, and her excitement rushed forward as Travis suddenly appeared on the screen.

"Hey, baby!" he said anxiously. "How are you?"

Tierra reached with one hand to adjust her own Web cam as she beamed back at him. "Hi, sweetheart. How are you?"

Travis nodded. "I'm good. I miss you, though. I miss you so much, Tierra!"

"I miss you, too!"

For twenty-five minutes, the couple chatted eagerly about everything and nothing. When Travis was tapped on the shoulder and advised that his time was up, it took every ounce of effort for Tierra not to burst into tears. Before their connection was disconnected, Travis called her name.

"I told you I had a surprise for you, right?"

"Yes..."

"Darling, I got my papers today. My transfer came through. I'll be leaving Afghanistan next week. They're sending me stateside, baby! I'll be in Texas, at Fort Hood, for the rest of my tour."

"Really?" Tierra exclaimed, her excitement at the prospect overwhelming.

"Two weeks, my darling, and I'll be able to hold you in my arms again."

The tears spilled down over Tierra's cheeks. "I love you," she said, wishing him well until the next time they spoke.

"Promise?" Travis asked, teasingly.

Tierra smiled, blowing him a kiss across the Internet lines. "For the rest of your natural-born days," she answered.

Winking, Travis blew her a kiss back. "I love you, too, Mrs. Stallion. I love you, too."

As the computer screen blinked, the connection lost, Tierra clutched her photo to her chest, her eyes closed as she fought back tears. Travis was coming home, and in that moment she couldn't imagine anything sweeter. He was coming home to her.

She kissed his photo, making plans for when she next saw her man. She'd given him her heart and had promised him forever. She'd made promises to a Stallion, and she intended to keep each and every one.

* * * * *